PREMONITIONS

JUDE WATSON

PUFFIN

PUFFIN BOOKS

Published by the Penguin Group
Penguin Books Ltd, 80 Strand, London WC2R 0RL, England
Penguin Group (USA), Inc., 375 Hudson Street, New York, New York 10014, USA
Penguin Books Australia Ltd, 250 Camberwell Road, Camberwell, Victoria 3124, Australia
Penguin Books Canada Ltd, 10 Alcorn Avenue, Toronto, Ontario, Canada M4V 3B2
Penguin Books India (P) Ltd, 11 Community Centre, Panchsheel Park, New Delhi – 110 017, India
Penguin Group (NZ), cnr Airborne and Rosedale Roads, Albany, Auckland 1310, New Zealand
Penguin Books (South Africa) (Pty) Ltd, 24 Sturdee Avenue, Rosebank 2196, South Africa

Penguin Books Ltd, Registered Offices: 80 Strand, London WC2R 0RL, England

www.penguin.com

First published in the USA by Scholastic Inc. 2004
First published in Great Britain in Puffin Books 2005
1

Made and printed in England by Clays Ltd, St Ives plc

British Library Cataloguing in Publication Data
A CIP catalogue record for this book is available from the British Library

ISBN 0–141–31921–6

They weren't the ones who could have stopped her.

I could have done that.

I was the one who saw the future.

I was the one who let her go.

ONE

I think I was a nice person before my mom died. I have a hard time connecting that person to the person I am now.

It's going on a year and a half since the accident, and I think I'm running out of leeway. People, like teachers, aren't giving me slack anymore.

One of these days, I'm going to have to decide on a personality.

I am mean to my best friend, Emily Carbonel, that day. And no, it isn't the first time. But I'm not the first person in her life to let her down.

So that's not why she disappears.

In Washington State it doesn't usually get hot in June, but today, the temperature is smack on ninety and the heat is making the air bounce. I just moved here from Maryland five months ago, so I'm used to humidity. I don't get why everyone is suddenly fainting from heat exhaustion. It just feels like summer to me. No school, and a bunch of people in shorts who really shouldn't be wearing them.

The only trouble is, my aunt Shay doesn't have air-conditioning. Most people don't on Beewick

Island. So I try to cool off the old-fashioned way — with a hose on my feet, in a shady spot in the backyard. When Emily drifts in and starts talking to me, it's too hot to make an excuse and go back inside, but it's too hot to listen to her, either.

It's one of the first days of summer vacation. Shay had suggested all sorts of fun summer programs to organize me, but I said no to all of them. She must have put in a secret call to my grandparents, because she targeted what used to be my interests before the accident. Photography camp? Swim club? Writing workshop? Summer job teaching art to kids?

No. No. No. No.

She gave up.

Emily doesn't have summer plans, either. Her parents haven't been able to get it together to do much for her this summer. They recently separated, and the whole thing is still pretty ugly. Emily had been accepted to a highly competitive computer camp in Seattle, but her parents fought over who would pay for it and if she'd live at her dad's full-time for the summer. They were so busy fighting that the deadline passed. So Emily's stuck with nothing to do all summer but pretend not to hear them fight on the phone and blame each other for the fact that Emily has nothing to do.

Emily must have some sort of built-in misery meter, because she attached herself to me the very first week I arrived on Beewick Island. I could tell she thought we were soul mates, since our parents had abandoned us. I wanted to scream at her that she was lucky her parents are still around and in her face. I wanted to point out that considering what had happened to me, *I* should have been the needy one. Instead, I just let her sit down at my table at lunch and unwrap her sprout sandwiches. I let us become friends.

I never would have picked Emily for a friend. First of all, we look stupid together. Emily is your standard tall blond, partial to tiny T-shirts and low-slung pants. I'm short, with acorn-color hair, and whatever interest in clothes I used to have has funneled down to finding jeans that are clean. Emily is practically plugged into her computer, and I don't even go online anymore because she's always messaging me when I just want to hang out and download some music. Her mode is permanently set on mope, and I don't need more depression in my life. She has a habit of not listening to you when you're talking, and this really pisses me off. I don't talk very much, and you'd think she'd make an effort to listen when I do.

Even though I have some sympathy for her, being with her sometimes just makes my brain scream for mercy. I consider myself in default mode, and she just happens to pop up in the friend department.

Like today. We sit on Shay's pink Adirondack chairs in the backyard, and I wait for her to get bored and go home.

"It is *so* hot," Emily says for about the thirty-sixth time. "Why don't we go into town? We could get ice cream and go to the library."

"I don't think I can handle the excitement," I reply.

Emily takes a swig of her Orangina. The smell of it makes my stomach turn. It is so hot. I lower my head and rest my cheek on my knees. I turn on the hose nozzle again and let the water wash over my bare toes. If we were really friends, I'd turn it on Emily, too. She's kicked off her sandals and even her little frosted toenails look sweaty.

"So will you come?" she asks.

I'm smelling orange soda and I feel woozy. "No. It's too hot."

"Maybe Diego would drive us."

I don't ask Diego for favors. "He's busy."

"Why don't you ask him?"

I think Emily has a secret crush on my cousin. There's probably some little old lady somewhere on Beewick Island who's the only one who doesn't, but I haven't met her yet.

Maybe Emily is trolling for a new boyfriend. One of the reasons she attached herself to me is because her old friends put her in cold storage. She'd dated Will Stein almost all of last year and dropped her friends like hot fries to spend every minute with him. Not that Emily told me this version, but the truth was pretty obvious. Then when Will broke up with her, they wanted to teach her a lesson, so they didn't take her back. They would have eventually, but Emily has a thing about rejection and just got frosty instead of wooing them back. Instead, she hung around me to show them she didn't care. Somehow, our friendship stuck, despite the fact that there was basically no reason for it to exist.

"Gracie?"

"What?"

"Are you my friend?"

It's the kind of question I hate. I look up at her, and that's when something happens. At first, I think it's just the heat playing tricks on me. It starts with something in the corner of my eye, a shadow that grows on the lawn. My heart starts to speed up, to patter in my chest like a hard rain. Because I know what's coming.

Suddenly, Emily looks different. Her short blond hair isn't swept back with clips anymore. It's matted to her forehead with sweat. The trees and lawn fade behind her, all the greens and blues, and I see her against a white background. I feel fear shimmer off her body in ripples. Then I can hear the sound of breathing in my ears. Only it's not mine, and it's not Emily's. It's someone else's.

Someone is looking at Emily.

She hears the breathing, but she doesn't look. She is afraid . . .

I close my eyes and tell the image to go away. *Go away. Go away.*

"All right."

Emily sounds hurt. I must have said the words out loud. When I open my eyes, she is clutching the Orangina bottle between her fingers and biting her lip. The sky is the same whitish blue, and the pine branches still look like they're drooping in the heat. The clips in her hair are yellow and pink. Shay's small house hunkers down on the hill, white clapboard and the windows with twelve tiny frames painted green. Everything is exactly the way it was.

Before I can say anything, Emily is walking away. She's really hurt and angry, but she keeps the empty Orangina bottle in her hand. She doesn't drop it on the lawn, like I would have done. Emily is a nice person.

I watch her cross the lawn. I should call her back, but I don't. She vanishes around the corner of the house and I put on my headphones. Within thirty seconds, I've forgotten about her.

I'm the last one to see her before she disappears.

TWO

You can drive from one tip of Beewick Island to the other in about an hour and across it in fifteen minutes. It's long and skinny, like the finger of a witch in a fairy tale. On a map, one skinny end is close to the mainland, and the other looks like it's making a break for Canada. The Olympic Mountains loom in the distance, blue and purple, their peaks snowcapped even in summer. The water in the bays is the color of blueberries, and there are fields of lavender that perfume the air if the wind is right. Seattle is about an hour away with no traffic, but there's always traffic.

It's not a bad place to live. Unless it's completely different from everything you've known, and you were never looking for a change.

So how did I end up here?

I don't think most impulses when you're fifteen are necessarily stupid, but sometimes it feels that way. Back in Maryland, I offered Jake Buscemi, who got the nickname "Scarface" in the sixth grade, twenty dollars to punch me. I really didn't expect him to take it. And I didn't expect the whole school to find out.

Oh, and another thing I didn't expect?

How much the punch would hurt.

The school called my grandparents, and they were a tad upset at the situation. I expected to be slammed right back into therapy, where I'd spent almost a year being coaxed by Dr. "Call Me Julie" Politsky to hug a stuffed panda. This was supposed to allow me to express my grief in a healthy, non-threatening, accepting atmosphere. The fact that I refused to make out with a stuffed animal indicated that I hadn't "fully processed my grief."

Oh, excuse me, Dr. Politsky. The next time your mom gets swiped by a jackknifing semi that turns her car into an accordion, I'll just toss a coot widdle stuffed panda in your lap.

So all my friends were really nice at first, and they were afraid to even mention my mom's name. In the beginning, that was a big relief. Then they started blushing whenever they mentioned their *own* moms, and they'd change the subject really fast. And soon I guess I was just too big of a drag to be around, because I started spending a lot of time in my room.

I could tell that everyone was waiting for me to *get on with it* and *process* and *find closure*. I tuned them out. I plugged into my headphones and filled up the empty space in my head with music. I didn't bother to listen to anyone anymore. I listened to songs instead, the same ones, over and over, until they made a groove in my mind that I could depend on.

But I guess I spooked my grandparents. Instead of more therapy, Mimi and Pop-Pop had a family conference and decided to follow through on my mom's original intention in her will, which was to have Aunt Shay be my guardian. The next thing I knew, I was yanked out of school during the midterm February break. The situation was deemed too serious to wait until June. I blinked, and suddenly I was on a plane to Seattle, clutching a roll of Tums and a noisy box of Tic Tacs, my grandmother's remedy for motion sickness.

My grandparents cried a bucket of tears at the airport, but I knew they were secretly happy that they could now return to playing golf all day instead of nagging me about my math homework. They'd raised three kids. They were done. It was apparent within weeks of their moving in with me — because the family agreed that after the tragedy I shouldn't be uprooted — that they realized they'd made a big mistake. There was even some attempt to find my father, which shows how seriously weird everything was at the time. My dad was a perfectly respectable D.C. lawyer before he went on a solo vacation to Santa Fe when I was three years old and never came back. He told my mom that he needed to "get clear." He promised to send child support. He sent one check. Then we never heard from him again.

Oh, sorry to interfere with your life crisis, Dad. Have a good one until you're dead.

So my dad was as gone as it gets, and my grandparents weren't equipped to handle me. They deserved to focus on nine-irons at this stage of their life, I guess. Uncle Owen lives half the time in D.C. and half the time in London. So that left Shay.

I'd only met Shay maybe a half-dozen times in my life, usually at some big, corny family reunion. She had a son, Diego, who was two years older than I was and completely uninterested in developing a cousinly relationship. It wasn't like we bonded over burgers on my mom's back porch, or kept up with each other on e-mail.

Once I moved to Beewick Island and into Shay's house, I was positive that if Mom had really known her sister instead of relying on telephone sisterly bonding and some hazy childhood memories, she would have changed her mind.

Shay is the complete opposite of Mom. For a scientist, she's an incredible dimwit. She's some kind of expert on wild grasses. *Very* exciting. She makes lists on Post-its that constantly fly off counters and flutter around the house like little fluorescent pink and yellow birds. They always get stuck on the bottom of your shoe. You peel them off and read things like *Buy oranges!* or *Learn Italian!*

She eats muffins the size of hats for breakfast. She cooks with butter. I can't count how many times she's yelled at dinner, "Oh, I forgot to make salad!"

Shay is round and curly-haired. She is a big fan of the drawstring-pants look. Her legs are strong from all the hiking she does, but she has a belly and flabby upper arms. She's always saying, "Oh, those extra ten pounds just turned into fifteen when I wasn't looking," or, "Help! I'm out of my fat pants and into my gross pants!" You'd think she'd stop baking muffins and cookies on Saturday mornings, wouldn't you?

Mom was a fresh-vegetable person. She was extremely healthy. She never embarrassed me. She never complained about something if she didn't plan to fix it.

I know that if this were a TV movie, I would fall into Shay's flabby upper arms and eat her blueberry muffins slathered with butter. I would take comfort from Shay's nurturing personality, her large breasts concealed in a series of Gap denim shirts, her insistence on calling me "sweetie" no matter how much I wince. I would tumble for her warmth, and slowly, painstakingly, find myself beginning to come alive again. Can't you see the misty reconciliation scene? Sob.

But this is real life, and I just feel pissed off.

I'm just about to go to sleep when the phone rings. I can hear Shay pick it up in the hallway.

I'm too tired at first to listen to what Shay's saying, but something about her voice wakes me up.

"I'll ask her. Hold on, sweetie," Shay says. Her voice has a gentleness to it, like she'd be holding the person's hand if she could.

A quick knock and she opens my door and stands in the doorway, the phone pressed against her chest. "Gracie, it's Emily's mom. Did you see Emily today?"

I know it immediately. It's like being hit in the chest with a baseball.

I know this question is not an opening into good news.

"We hung out for a while in the backyard," I say.

The answer sounds empty.

I feel empty. Everything has drained out of me.

Because I know what's coming.

"Do you remember what time it was?" Shay asks.

I think back. "After lunch. About two o'clock, I guess."

"Did she say where she was going?"

Remember. You have to remember.

But I remember stupid details, like the smell of oranges, and Emily's toenail polish, and her finger tapping against the glass of the bottle. I hear that tap in my head, and it grows, and it drowns everything out.

"I think she wanted to get ice cream, but I didn't want to go to town."

Shay looks more concerned, if that's possible. "Did Emily walk to town?"

"I don't know. She just left."

I know that's not the answer anyone wants to hear.

It's not the one I want to say.

But it's all I have.

I know Emily's mother isn't panicking for nothing. It isn't like Emily to stay out late. I know why her mother is worried. She should be worried. We should all be worried.

Shay listens on the phone, then says, "Of course, right away." She hangs up but doesn't put down the phone. She grips it and takes a breath.

"The Carbonels want us to come over. They want to talk to you about Emily. They think you're the last person to talk to her. She hasn't come home."

The night is warm. The windows are open. I'm shivering, and trying to hide it from Shay.

Emily's eyes shut tight.

The sound of someone breathing.

Shay is waiting for me to move, and I'm not moving, because I know with cold certainty that everything I saw was true.

It's happening again, and I can't stop it.

I don't want this. I never wanted this. I just want it to go away.

I didn't want to see a red bloom of a stain spreading on my Uncle Owen's chest, on his white shirt. Two days later, he had a tear in his aorta and almost died. In eighth grade, I didn't want to see that Hannah Bascomb was afraid of her own father, or the reasons she was. I didn't want to know the results of our neighbor Mrs. Shale's biopsy before she did.

It's like people are bleeding in front of me, and I can't move to help them.

I have too much sorrow crowding my heart as it is.

The worst possible thing has happened to me. I don't have room inside me to care about it happening to anybody else.

But I get up and get dressed.

THREE

Every light in Emily's house must be on, as if all that light could shine out to tell her it's okay to come home. I'm surprised when Mr. Carbonel answers the door. He hasn't stepped foot in the house in months. He must have driven from Seattle as soon as they decided Emily was missing. It must be really bad if both of Emily's parents are willing to be in the same room together.

Shay gives him a hug, patting his shoulder like he's a kid. She's known both Carbonels for years, and I think she's even closer to Emily's dad than her mom. Emily's mom is something of a head case.

We walk into the living room. I've never actually sat down in the living room before; it's just a pass-through on the way to the kitchen for Emily and me. It doesn't invite lounging, anyway. There's a 1950s-style orange couch that looks toxic, and a coffee table shaped like a surfboard. Mrs. Carbonel painted one of the walls violet and another wall pink. It doesn't work.

Mrs. Carbonel sits on the couch. She's perched on the edge, as if the phone will ring any second and she'll need to answer it. The phone is lying right next to her on the cushion. Even though it's almost midnight, everybody is still dressed, down to their shoes.

A stranger is sitting in the only comfortable chair in the room, an armchair upholstered in maroon leather. He rises when we come in. Mrs. Carbonel introduces him as Detective Joe Fusilli. He has a big nose and dark eyes that don't seem to have any expression at all. The bags underneath them look like suitcases packed for a six-week trip.

I get a quick flash from him. Sometimes this happens. I get sadness from him, sadness that lies buried underneath everything that's inside him that has to do with the job. I see him bending over someone, someone he loves, who stares blankly out the window.

Shay nods a hello. I think she might have smiled at his name if the situation had been different. It isn't often you meet a detective named after corkscrew pasta.

Shay and I sit down on the couch. Mrs. Carbonel leans forward, her hands clasped between her legs. Every so often, she catches them between her knees and squeezes. Mr. Carbonel sits on the other chair. He's a stocky man with big shoulders and arms and a silver beard. I've met him maybe four times, and each time, I've picked up waves of guilt when he looked at Emily. Now I notice that he never looks at his ex-wife.

The worry in this room is like a heavy blanket on a warm day. I can feel it pressing against me, and I want to kick it free.

"Gracie, did Emily seem upset today?" Mrs. Carbonel asks.

I remembered her face as she walked away. "No."

Joe Fusilli's dark eyes are on me. I decide to break my usual habit and tell the truth. It seems called for.

"Well, I wouldn't say she was really upset. But she wasn't happy when I wouldn't go to town with her. It was too hot."

"Do you think she went by herself?" Mrs. Carbonel continues.

"I don't know," I say. "I'm sorry."

Mrs. Carbonel's mouth twists, and she looks away.

Detective Fusilli speaks up. "Gracie, do you remember what Emily was wearing?"

"Sure. A white T-shirt and yellow capri pants. They have tiny pink flowers on them. And brown sandals. The kind you can hike in. Merrell's."

Mrs. Carbonel nods at the detective like a good student, as if that's what she's told him, too. As if we all give him the right answers, he'll find her.

He writes in his notebook. "Did Emily seem to have anything special on her mind?"

"Nothing in particular," I say.

"What did you talk about?"

"How hot it was, basically," I say.

"What about other times?" Detective Fusilli asks. "Did Emily ever talk about running away?"

"No."

I was sure of that. No matter how much she trashed her parents, she never talked about leaving.

"How about a boyfriend?"

I shake my head.

"A crush?"

I shake my head again. "Emily never talked about boys."

Detective Fusilli looks skeptical. "Oh?"

"Really," I say. I'm seriously annoyed now. I want to tell him to think about it a minute. Doesn't it occur to him that Emily and I might have other things on our minds? Like the fact that her parents are flakes and I don't have any?

"Did Emily ever mention having a Net buddy? Someone she met on the Internet?"

"She e-mailed some people, sure," I say. "I don't know who they are, though."

"Do you think she'd meet one of them without telling you, or her parents?"

I think about this. One thing about Emily, she follows the rules. "I don't know. I don't think so."

Mrs. Carbonel squeezes her hands between her knees again. "We can't find her laptop," she says to Shay. "She took it."

"Did she have the laptop when you saw her, Gracie?" Detective Fusilli asks.

I shake my head. So Emily must have gone home to get it.

"Is anything else missing?" Shay asks.

"No. No clothes or anything." Mrs. Carbonel starts to cry. "She was upset that she didn't get to go to that camp . . ." She looks at Mr. Carbonel for the first time. "If you would have agreed to exchange summer for school breaks —"

"I *did* agree," Mr. Carbonel says. "You wouldn't agree to Christmas —"

"You know we were planning a trip to Arizona!"

"I was going to send the check!"

"After the deadline!" Mrs. Carbonel's voice rises sharply and ends on a sob. She looks at Mr. Carbonel as if she hates him, and I guess she does. The anger between them could fill up six houses. No wonder he had to move out. There's no room to live in this house. I'm finding it hard to breathe. Had all this anger squeezed Emily out, too?

"Let's try to calm down," Detective Fusilli says. "She's only been gone eleven hours. She could come home."

I know he doesn't believe it. I can see the dread. It is his enemy. It is lead in his bones. The feeling is familiar to him, it is part of the job, but he hates it.

"It's midnight and she's out there somewhere," Mrs. Carbonel says. "Can't you do something?"

"We're on alert," Detective Fusilli says. He stands up. "What that means is that every cop in the state is looking. If you think of anything, call me. If she gets home, call me. If you remember anything, call me. Even if it's the middle of the night."

"You're leaving?" Mrs. Carbonel asks, her voice rising in panic. "You're just going to leave?"

"I'm going to get to work and find your daughter." The detective's voice is soft now. He feels the dread moving up to his throat, and he wants out of here, he wants to find the kid, and he's saying, *Please, let her be alive.*

Mr. and Mrs. Carbonel nod. I can see they want to believe in Detective Fusilli's competence so badly. Mr. Carbonel rises and shows the detective to the door.

We all stare at the carpet. "Why don't I make some tea?" Shay asks. No one answers, so she goes in the kitchen. I hear her filling the kettle.

"We did this to her, Rocky," Mrs. Carbonel says. She doesn't sound angry anymore. She sounds worse.

"Yeah," Mr. Carbonel says. "I know."

It's like I'm not in the room.

Joe Fusilli left some of his dread behind. I can

feel the weight of it settle inside me, anchor me to the chair.

Emily's parents feel guilty. But they weren't the one who could have stopped her.

I was the one who could have done that.

I was the one who saw her future.

I was the one who let her go.

FOUR

We don't talk on the ride home. I'm thinking about my answers to the detective's questions. How many times had I said *I don't know*? Had I really known Emily all that well? Had I ever really listened to her? Or was I too busy listening to my own head?

I wish I'd turned the hose on her feet, too.

Shay pulls into the driveway. She turns off the car, but she doesn't move. "Gracie, is there anything you didn't want to say in front of Emily's parents?"

"What do you mean?"

"I don't know. Something Emily might have said, or done, and you don't want to get her in trouble."

"That would be pretty stupid of me," I say. "She's pretty much in the worst trouble I can imagine right now."

"Yeah. If you want to talk —"

"There's nothing to talk about," I say, shouldering open my door. Which, I admit, is a pretty stupid thing to say, considering my best-friend-by-default is missing. But what's the good of talking about anything? Adults just don't get it. They think that expressing your feelings makes them go away.

Next, Shay would be tossing stuffed animals at me to hug.

Shay gets out of the car. It's cooler now. The heat of the day has dissolved into a breeze that makes the pines whisper.

"I don't think I can sleep yet," Shay says as she opens the front door. "Do you want to share some cookies and milk? Or I could make omelettes."

"Do you always think you can fix things with food?" I ask. I'm tired, and the question comes out snottier than I meant it to. The truth is, I'm so stuffed full of the emotion I felt at the Carbonel house I feel sick.

Shay looks hurt for a minute. She runs a hand through her springy hair and takes a breath. I can tell she's searching for the right thing to say. "No," she says finally.

"I think I'll just go to bed," I say.

"All right, sweetie," Shay says, but I'm already walking down the hall.

I pull on a big T-shirt and climb into bed. My room is tiny, but I don't mind. There's something about it that makes me feel safe. My mom used to say, "Climb into your nest," when I was a little kid, and pull up the blankets and mound the pillows and stuffed animals around me. This room reminds me of that, in a way.

It used to be a mud room, a sort of summer porch in the back of the house. Shay and Diego went to some trouble to fix it up, I guess. Shay had winterized it. They painted the floor dark blue and the windowsills yellow. Shay bought an old dresser and painted it white. My bed has a patchwork quilt with moons on it. White gauzy curtains hang at the windows now, because it's summer, but in winter Shay had hung thick velvet drapes to keep out drafts. Now that's it's warm I can open the windows all the way, and hear all the night noises outside. I can smell the Sound and hear the foghorns. Sometimes I feel I'm on a big liner, out in the middle of the ocean. That's how far away I feel.

I reach for my mp3 player. I've filled it with songs my mom loved, dopey songs I never listened to when she was around. We used to have a serious difference in musical tastes. But now when my head is full of things I don't want to think about, which is most of the time, I just drown them out. If something plays in my head, I can't hear what I'm thinking. Tonight I listen to Boy George singing "Karma Chameleon."

But I can't stop thinking about the dread I'd seen in Joe Fusilli. It wasn't in his eyes, or his face, or things he said. It was there inside him.

He doesn't think Emily is coming home tonight. I don't think so, either.

This is how it started.

When I was ten, I went to the shore with my

best friend, Annie Keegan, and her three brothers. Her mom set up the cooler and blanket and the chairs, and we all ran into the ocean. Mrs. Keegan yelled for us to wait for her, but we pretended we didn't hear her over the wind and the seagulls.

I remember how high the waves were, but I didn't want Annie's brothers to tease me about being a wimp, so I waded right in. I was doing okay until I misjudged a wave. I remember being taken over by the wave, how I tumbled and tumbled, how I tried to swim and couldn't. The force of the wave was incredible. I couldn't get my head above water. Then when I did, another wave was coming, and that one hit me, too. I swallowed water and I suddenly knew I was drowning. I don't remember that part very clearly, just that things slowed down, but I still couldn't get out of the grip of the wave.

The next thing I knew, I was on the beach. I heard a voice clearly in my head, a voice I didn't recognize. It was saying, *Come on, come on, come on, come on.* I opened my eyes. A lifeguard was looking down at me. *Oh please oh please oh please* . . . She had blue eyes that were filled with fear. Her freckles stood out against her tan like blotches.

I saw the relief on her face and I also *felt* it. It flooded my body, like it was inside me. Then I started to cough and threw up on her leg.

Mrs. Keegan wrapped me in a towel and hugged me. I remember that so clearly. How scared everyone looked, how the lifeguard sagged down on the sand, how the other lifeguards clustered around her and me. I remember Mrs. Keegan's hair blowing into my mouth, and that it tasted like salt. Everything looked different, somehow, like the world was sharper than it had been. Everything was louder. I could feel the day like it had weight, like I could feel seconds passing like air currents, like I could cup my hands and collect moments like water.

Then I sat on the blanket for a while, and drank some water, and ate a chocolate chip cookie, and things shifted again, and I felt normal.

Mrs. Keegan asked me if I was still scared. I said no. Mrs. Keegan smiled and said she thought the lifeguard had been more scared than I was. She said the lifeguard had to go home — it had been her first day on the job.

Somehow I'd already known that. I figured I'd overheard someone saying it. I said something about how her voice had called me back, saying, *come on, come on* and *please please please . . .*

Mrs. Keegan shook her head. "The lifeguard never said anything. She was trying to resuscitate you. Nobody said anything. We were all frozen. Everything went very quiet. I think even the sea-gulls stopped squawking."

I stopped asking questions and chewed on this along with my cookie. The lifeguard hadn't spoken, but I'd heard her voice. I didn't know what to make of that, so I just hoped I wouldn't get in trouble when I got home for not listening to Mrs. Keegan and running into the surf.

I didn't realize everything that had changed until later, until after I began to see things and feel things. It's hard to explain. People talk, and I hear what they're saying, but I also see something in a flash, like a digital photograph starting out jagged and then filling in.

I finally told Mom. It took her a while to accept it. Then after I told her that something was wrong in Uncle Owen's chest and two days later he was in the ER, she got serious. She called a couple of places and thought about getting me tested, but neither of us wanted to do that. I didn't want it to be real, somehow. I don't think Mom did, either. She was a very practical person. I think she just wanted it to go away. I couldn't blame her. So did I.

I still do.

I turn up the music. I don't want to think about where Emily is. I don't want to know what's happening to her. It will be a long time before I'm able to close my eyes.

I'm afraid of what I'll see if I do.

FIVE

I don't remember falling asleep, but when I wake up at five A.M., I know I'm not getting back to sleep. I never do. My face is wet, and so are the ends of my hair, which is clinging to the back of my neck. I know I've been crying in my dreams again. I'm shaking and I pull a sweater on over my T-shirt.

I asked her not to go.

She said, *Did you see something?*

No, I said. *Not like that. It's just . . . a feeling. I'm afraid something will happen.*

She had smiled. *I'll be back tomorrow. I'm just flying down to take a deposition.*

I didn't say anything. That was the moment. That was when I could have said, *don't go.* I could have begged. I could have pitched a fit. I could have lied and said I saw a vision of her plane crashing.

I'll call you when I land, she said.

She called from her cell phone, right from the plane while it was on the runway. She'd landed safely. The weather was clear in West Palm. After the deposition, she was hoping to take a walk on the beach. She wished I was with her — it was December, and it was seventy-five degrees. She wanted pompano for dinner. She'd never had pompano.

And key lime pie, I said.

I had hung up the phone, feeling relieved. And then I couldn't seem to figure out what to do with the day. Rosie, the friend of my mom's who was staying with me, made me a sandwich. I sat in front of the TV and ate it. It stuck in my throat and it was hard to swallow.

I started to choke. I choked and choked. I couldn't breathe. Rosie came running to help.

There was nothing in my mouth to choke on.

I ran to the phone. I called her cell, my fingers stabbing the buttons. Her cell phone had no service.

For the next four hours, I kept dialing the number, over and over and over. I just sat on the couch, dialing, while Rosie peeked in the room at me, a worried expression on her face. She kept saying, *I'm sure everything is fine,* and I kept dialing, not even bothering to answer her.

The next thing I knew, my grandparents were at the door. They lived two hours away, and as soon as I saw them, I knew. I put my hands over my ears and screamed. I screamed and screamed.

I am still, somewhere in my head, screaming.

They tried to keep the details from me, but you find out. A bit here, a bit there, a question you don't want to ask but do.

Don't think about it. Don't think about how it happened. Don't think about it.

I turn on all the lights. Better.

I tiptoe out into the short hallway. The house is so quiet. Even the birds haven't woken up yet. I push open the door to the kitchen. I know just how much to push the door so that it doesn't squeak. I squeeze in through the gap.

I turn on the kitchen light and sit at the table. It's an old wood table, with knotholes and wide planks. I put my hands on the wood. I stick my fingers in the knotholes. Sometimes feeling things helps. After Mom died, I couldn't understand how a table could still feel so solid. I felt like the whole world was dissolving and I would fall through the edges of things. Nothing had seemed real.

I rest my cheek against the table. It is so strange to live without touch. Mom touched my hair as she walked by. She hugged me. She scratched my feet while we watched TV. She kissed my forehead. Shay doesn't touch me much because I flinch when she does.

If only, I think, the missing her would go away. Then maybe I could figure out how to live with everything else. The fear that I'll always be like this is the worst.

The door squeaks behind me. I don't know how she does it. But Shay always knows when I'm up. I sit up straight, but I don't turn to face her. I don't want to see anyone, not yet, not while I'm afraid.

I hear her get out the milk and pour it into a pan. I hear her rummage for cups. I hear the paper rattling as she unwraps the chocolate.

By the time I can smell the milk, I'm calmer. Shay puts a cup down in front of me. It is a blue cup with a green dot on the handle for my thumb to rest on. It's my favorite. I haven't told her that, but she knows.

She breaks off a piece of chocolate and puts it in the bottom of the cup. She puts a spoon and a napkin near my hand. Then she pours the frothy warm milk into my cup. I watch the milk swirl around the chocolate. Within a few seconds, I can see curls of melted chocolate in the milk.

Shay pours her own milk. We stir, the spoons tinkling softly. We take our first sip. The warmth and the sweetness fill my mouth.

The first time Shay made me hot chocolate her way, I had been shaking and crying. It's hard to describe the feeling — it's panic and pain and rage all mixed together, and it sent me shooting from my bed without thought, moving anywhere to get rid of what I was feeling. She had put a hand on my shoulder, and I had jerked my shoulder away. She had asked me if I wanted to talk, and I had said no, said it very loud and very strong and very mean. I had told her to go away and leave me alone.

When she didn't leave, when I heard her rustling around the kitchen, I didn't turn around. I wouldn't give an inch. I didn't care what she was doing, I didn't want anything she had to give. I almost didn't drink what she put down in front of me. Then I had taken the tiniest of sips, resolving not to finish it, not to give her the satisfaction. But there was something about the way she sat there, sipping her own drink, that had calmed me. She hadn't tried to talk. She hadn't looked at me. She had looked out at the gathering light. I had finished the hot chocolate. I was suddenly grateful for the kitchen lights, the blue cup, the silence.

I didn't know how to say thank you. So I washed the cups instead, and the milk pan. She waited at the table. And then we went back to our beds, where I guess we both stared into space until it was time to get up.

That had set the pattern. Shay doesn't try to touch me. She doesn't speak. She just comes and keeps me company until morning starts.

The birds start to make a racket. The light starts out black and turns blue. I've never seen anything like it before. In Maryland, the day just gets lighter. Here, it gets bluer. I wonder where Emily is.

I drain the chocolate, feeling guilty at how good it tastes. And I wonder if I can stand one more death.

SIX

No news?

No news.

It goes on like that for days.

I have nothing to do but wait. Shay goes to work. There's a line between her eyebrows now when she looks at me. I know that she wants to sit down and have a talk. I know exactly what she's thinking, and it's not because I can read her mind.

I do a lot of loud dishwashing, so Shay can't start a conversation. I clean my closet and rearrange my bookshelves. I appear busy whenever she's home, and I lay around when she's gone.

I try to remember something else — anything else — about Emily.

I get nothing.

Sometimes all I remember is how much I wanted her to go away.

I do everything in a Novocaine-type way that I remember from the period right after Mom's funeral. Someone dies, and for a while you do nothing. You don't even notice anything except pain. You see strangers, people on the street, people passing in cars, and you feel like screaming at them. *What are you doing? My mother is dead!*

But then, incredibly, days follow each other, and there is life-stuff to do. My grandparents moved into the house so that I could finish out my freshman year. That was really nice of them. But the only bedroom they could use was Mom's, so we had to pack some of her things away. They were careful to leave plenty of her things around — I'm sure that was Dr. Politsky's advice, because she counseled us during the "transitions." So they cleaned out drawers and closets, but they left Mom's perfume bottles on the dresser and her jewelry in the little blue-and-white bowls she used to hold her earrings. That was nice of them, too, I guess. I guess I would have felt worse if they gave every-thing away, right away, or put things into storage. That came later.

So they moved in, and there were groceries to buy, and I had to show them where the recycling went, and how to use the washing machine, and which place had the good bread and which place had the good tomatoes. I had to do these things, so I did them. But I felt like everything was frozen, and every little act took way too much energy. I took tiny steps and moved in small ways. I tried not to speak.

My freshman year ended, and my grandparents decided that since I still wasn't doing so well, they should move to my town permanently so I could finish out high school. But it didn't matter if I stayed where I was. Nobody seemed to realize that.

Christmas was the worst. We put up a tree and we gave one another presents. When it got really unbearable, we mutually agreed without speaking that we would watch TV constantly instead of trying to communicate. And I slid, from December to January, into a black place that seemed worse than the first days after the accident.

It was a bad place to be.

Now reminds me of then, and that scares me. It should make me feel better, it should make me see how far I've come in only five months. I didn't realize I'd gotten better, but I had. Instead it just shows me that I can slide backward so easily, right down the slope, back into where I was — a wasteland of ice.

"Hey," Diego says.

"Hey," I say.

This counts as a typical conversation with Diego. When I think of my cousin, I picture the back of his head. Usually because he's heading out the door. I've lived here for almost five months, and he's gone through a string of girlfriends, all of them named Jessica. Or maybe it just seems that way. Currently he's engaged in marathon phone sessions with a girl named Marigold. Yes, Marigold.

I'm sitting between my bed and the wall. I heard the screen door slam, and I knew Diego was home from his summer job with a landscaping crew. I was hoping that he'd figure no one was home and leave me alone, but for some reason Diego always seeks me out to say hello before he disappears into the glow of his laptop. Shay probably makes him.

To my surprise, Diego crouches down beside me and slides into a sitting position. His legs are too long, so he props them up against the wall. He smells like freshly mown grass, and I see a few stray green spears on his bare shins. I notice that Diego is already tan. He's got dark skin, inherited from his Spanish father, I guess. I never asked him about his father, and I haven't asked Shay. No one in the family knows anything about what happened to Shay in Spain. They only know that she lived in Spain for a year and came back pregnant.

Shay told everyone she didn't want to discuss it and didn't want to answer questions. She instructed them that they were to accept and love her baby. Everyone in the family kept their mouths shut for once, and obeyed.

I wonder if even Diego knows the story. In a way, his father is even more of a mystery than mine.

Diego gives me a sidelong look. He is incredibly handsome. He's got those dark eyes that stupid girls call "soulful." No wonder he has a string of Jessicas.

I guess I'm staring, because Diego inches back a little, like I have something contagious. Then he drums his fingers on the floor.

"I got something for you," he says. He sounds nervous.

"Okay," I say cautiously.

He slides a book over. He was keeping it hidden by his side. I lean over and read the title: *Psychic Power Points: How to Nurture, Develop, and Utilize Your Own Hidden Intuitive Abilities.*

My blood pounds in my head. I can feel my face turning red. I didn't know that Diego knew about me. His big-mouth mother must have told him.

By the way, your cousin Gracie is going to move in with us. We'll have to feed her, clothe her, give up our summer porch, and include her in dinner-table conversation. And did I mention this? She's a wacko.

I slide the book back across the floorboards at him with such force it hits his leg harder than I meant it to. He looks at me, shocked. He's pissed off, too, I can tell. We stare at each other for a minute. After having basically no contact except "please pass the salt" for five months, it's hard to handle our first fight.

"Don't tell me," Diego says with a twist to his mouth. "You've read it already?"

"This," I say, putting my fist on the book, "is none of your business."

"Okay," Diego says. He's nodding, but I can tell

it's not because he's agreeing, he's just trying to figure out the next thing to say. "That's fine. Nothing about you is my business, right? Except that you live in my house and are in my face."

I draw up my knees against my chest. For some reason, what he says hurts me. I didn't think I knew Diego well enough to allow him to hurt my feelings. "It's not my choice, in case you haven't noticed," I throw back at him.

"Gracie," he says in a nicer tone. It's weird to hear my name come out of his mouth. He never uses my name. He just says "hey."

"What I mean is," he continues, "ever since Emily disappeared, you've been holed up in here, and it's obvious that you're spooked about something."

"Maybe I'm spooked because she disappeared into thin air?" I suggest.

"Mom thinks you might know something about it," Diego says, which makes me furious again, just when I'm starting to calm down. "I don't mean you're hiding something," he says quickly. "She thinks maybe you saw something . . . I mean, in your head."

"Well, I didn't."

"Whatever." I can't tell whether Diego doesn't believe me, or whether he really doesn't care. "But if that's true, I thought maybe if you knew how to access that, you could learn something that could help Emily. Or not be scared anymore, at least."

My head jerks up. *Scared*. How had Diego known that?

Diego sighs, like this conversation is just too heavy for him to process. He gets up and walks out. No doubt Marigold is panting for his attention. After I'm sure he's gone all the way down the hall, I pick up the book.

When a kid disappears, your town gets smaller. Neighbors bring things and leave them on the doorstep. People tie yellow ribbons on trees. Posters go up in every shop. Strangers hit their knees at night with one name on their lips. In every gaze, there is that awareness, that shock that a kid has been lured and taken, in the middle of a slow summer day. Your town becomes better than it was, and everyone says, *how could it happen here?* Forgetting the things that happen all the time — the divorces, the dad who hits mom, the depressions, the alcoholics who send their kids to school with a bag of popcorn instead of a sandwich. It happens everywhere, but suddenly, how could it happen here?

I think of the strain on the faces of Emily's parents. I think of how that phone sat on the cushion. How Emily's mother's hands kept kneading the material of her pants. How Emily's father's broad chest seemed to have caved in.

I think of Emily against that white background, sweaty and scared.

I look at the book in my lap.

I don't want to open myself up to this darkness, this dread. I don't want to see any further, any deeper, than I already have.

But since I can't do nothing, this is the least I can do.

SEVEN

The next morning is Saturday, Diego's day off. He's at the breakfast table, chomping his way through Shay's homemade granola, when I stop in front of him. I put the book down on the table.

"It says that psychics can get flashes from touching things that a missing person owned," I say. "I've never actually tried to *get* the visions. I've always tried to *avoid* them."

He nods slowly, still chewing, his liquid eyes on my face.

"I was wondering if you'd give me a ride to Emily's house," I say really fast, before I lose my nerve.

He stands up, still shoveling the last of his cereal in his mouth. The spoon hits his bowl with a loud clang. "Let's go."

Diego must have taken a page from Shay's rule book, because he doesn't say anything on the drive to Emily's. He's probably waiting for me to say something. I'm sure an apology is in order, for example, but I'm too nervous to give one, and I'm not sure what I'd be apologizing for, anyway. For hitting him with a book? For moving into his house in the first place?

We don't have to knock on the door. It opens immediately, and Mrs. Carbonel practically grabs us by our collars.

"Do you know anything?" she asks.

Quickly, we shake our heads. The disappointment on her face is so painful to see that I actually take a step back. Her eyes have purple smudges under them, and her hair is completely matted on one side. Mrs. Carbonel always looked a little sad to me. Now she looks insane. She was always thin, but her khaki shorts are hanging off her hips. I think she's wearing the T-shirt she slept in. It looks creased, and there's a stain on it that looks like coffee.

She steps away from the door listlessly, as if it doesn't matter why we're here now. She goes right to the sofa and sits. The phone still lies on the cushion next to her.

"I was wondering if I could see Emily's room," I say. I've been trying to think of a reason the whole way over. I don't want to tell Mrs. Carbonel why I want to. I can't imagine what she'd think if I told her the truth. I can't imagine how furious she'd be at me. I would be furious at me, if I were her.

"Why?" Mrs. Carbonel asks. I'm not sure if she really is interested in the answer. Even though we're in the room, she's busy listening to something else going on in her head. I know that look.

The world isn't real to her now. It won't be real to her until her daughter walks through the door.

I'd thought on the way over to say that I wanted to borrow something of Emily's, something to remember her, but suddenly, that seems really stupid. It would seem like I was thinking she was dead.

Then I thought I'd say I'd left something of mine in her room. But suddenly that seems awful, too. How could I be thinking about a missing T-shirt or a CD when Emily is gone?

So instead I just stand there like an idiot.

That's when Diego steps in. "Gracie misses Emily," he says. "Would you mind if she just spent a little time in Emily's room?"

Mrs. Carbonel's eyes fill with tears. "Oh, sweetheart." She leaps up from the sofa and hugs me. She rocks me back and forth. "Oh, sweetheart," she says again, this time into my hair. "Of course you miss her, too."

Mrs. Carbonel hugs me really hard, so hard I can feel her breastbone. It almost hurts, but I don't move. I hug her back, swallowing against a huge lump in my throat. The only thing that keeps me from crying along with her is not wanting Diego to see it. I wish I could pass just a little relief from my body into hers, but I don't have any to give.

Mrs. Carbonel turns away, rubbing at her eyes with a tissue. "Go ahead," she says.

"Can I make you some tea?" Diego asks. His

mother's son, that's for sure. If I leave him in the kitchen too long, he'll be baking muffins.

I walk into Emily's room. I've been here plenty of times. Without Emily, it's just a room. A bed with a pink quilt. A dresser, a chair, a bookcase.

What should I pick? I'm not sure it matters. I pick up her hairbrush and put it down. I open the closet, but nothing seems right. I run my fingers along her clothes.

I move to her dresser and pick up a bracelet. I don't think I've ever seen her wear it. Then I see a framed photograph. It is of Emily at the beach, probably taken just this past winter, because she's wearing a jacket and a bright striped wool scarf that I recognize. She's grinning at whoever is behind the camera, and somehow I know it's her father, on one of the weekends they spend together, because there is something a little too giddy about her smile. The light is just perfect. It's one of those shots, one out of twenty-six on the roll, that you just get right. The light in Emily's eyes, the light on the water, the striped scarf against the gray sky and rocks on the beach.

I pick it up and run my finger along Emily's cheek.

The images come at first in pieces that shimmer. Somehow this time I can remain outside of the fear I feel. I know what I'm seeing, and I can concentrate enough so I can see it clearly, or as clearly as I can.

Emily. Emily and water.

Emily is moving, up and down. A boat. The boat is hitting waves, hard, ramming down in a trough of a wave and then grinding up a curl.

Emily is not afraid. She is laughing at the bucking boat.

Then the water changes.

It is a waterfall I see now, a beautiful blue waterfall with sunlight glinting on the spray. It is the biggest waterfall I've ever seen, but oddly, there is no sound now, where before I could hear the slam of the boat and hear Emily's laughter.

Then I see something I don't understand. Quick flashes of an object. It is cubelike, white, and flames shoot out of it. It frightens me. Fear settles in my bones and I feel it grow. It expands to fill the space between my ribs and my stomach and my throat. I feel the scream in my throat.

"Gracie!"

Diego is kneeling in front of me, and I'm sitting on the floor. It takes what feels like long seconds to focus on his face.

"What is it?" he asks. "What did you see?"

"What?" I croak.

"We heard you yell," he says.

Mrs. Carbonel is holding a mug of tea. "What's going on?" she asks, frowning.

I drop my head in my hands. I need to make sense of this before I say anything. But Mrs. Carbonel drops down on the rug and leans toward me. "Gracie, tell me what's happening this instant."

I hear the panic in her voice, and the fear, and I say in a voice that doesn't sound like me, "Sometimes I see things."

I lift my head. Mrs. Carbonel looks at Diego.

"Gracie has psychic abilities," he says. "We thought maybe she could help. I'm sorry, we didn't —"

Mrs. Carbonel's eyes widen as she takes this in. Then she leans forward. Her gaze is burning with hunger.

"Tell me." Mrs. Carbonel grabs my knee with her free hand. "Tell me what you saw."

I tell her the best news I can. "She's alive," I say.

Mrs. Carbonel jerks and cries out. The tea spills on her bare knee. She begins to sob. Her face is so open, so naked. She sits perfectly still, but her whole body shakes with each violent sob.

Diego disappears, running. He comes back in a few seconds with a washcloth. He takes the mug of tea out of Mrs. Carbonel's hand and presses the cold washcloth on her leg where the hot tea had spilled. Mrs. Carbonel doesn't even notice.

"Tell me," she says.

"She left with someone she trusts," I say. "She

wasn't afraid. She was in a boat. Then I saw a water-fall."

"What else?" Mrs. Carbonel asks, her voice urgent now.

I can't tell her about the white cube and the flames. I know it would be too much. I just can't do it.

"That's all," I say.

Rocky Carbonel is suddenly in the doorway. "What's going on?"

Mrs. Carbonel stands up. Her skin is so tight against her bones. It's the oddest smile I've ever seen, ecstatic, delivered. "She's alive, Rocky."

She walks across the room and grabs his hands. "She's alive. Gracie saw her . . . in a vision . . . Gracie saw her in a boat. She saw her! And she isn't afraid! That's what broke me, Rocky, the thought of her being afraid. . . ."

I feel cold inside. Emily *is* afraid. I remember back to the first vision. However she left, things are different now.

Slowly, Rocky Carbonel's face changes. Hardens. He looks at me with such anger it feels as though he's shoved me up against a wall.

"What are you doing to her?" he says to me. "Get out."

I reach out a hand to Diego. "Mr. Carbonel, Gracie is just trying to help," Diego says.

"Get her out of here," Mr. Carbonel says, each word a rock thrown at my head. He looks at his ex-wife. "What's the matter with you?"

"She's alive," Mrs. Carbonel says, her face set in the same smiling grimace, tears running down her face. "She's alive."

Gently, as though I'm a newborn colt, Diego helps me up from the floor. My legs don't work right. He leads me out of Emily's bedroom, Rocky Carbonel's furious gaze following us.

The front door shuts quietly behind us. I remember why I hate having what some people call a gift. It is not a gift and never has been. It is ten tons of concrete on my back. It is every misery in the world. It's inside of me, and I can never get rid of it.

It will never go away.

EIGHT

Diego and Shay have this whole shared language that I'm not part of, a shorthand I remember from my relationship with my mom. All Mom had to do was say, "I'll take a Pooka-sized slice," and I'd know that she meant an extra-big piece of cake. Our old dog, Pooka, was about the size of a handbag, but she could eat twice her weight in one sitting.

In other words, a family has shorthand. When you lose your family, you lose that. You just can't walk into another family and pick it up, either. Shay bent over backward to include me. If she and Diego said something I didn't get, she'd tell this anecdote about how it came about, and I'd listen politely, but the whole explanation is so lame, because the thing about family shorthand is, you had to be there. I wasn't there with Shay and Diego. And the person I was there with once, through a million memories, isn't with me anymore. So I don't have a shorthand I can ever say out loud, ever again. You would think when you lose your family, you just lose love, but guess what? You lose a whole vocabulary.

In other words, Diego and Shay are close. So I'm surprised when Diego doesn't tell Shay what happened at the Carbonels. I can tell because there's nothing in the air between us, no more than usual, anyway.

Shay makes pasta with broccoli that night. She puts the bowl on the table and leans over to smell it. Then she takes a piece of broccoli in her fingers and eats it. I don't know why she can't wait until she puts it on a plate.

"Geesh," she says. "It's a good thing we're not having visitors tonight. I might have overdone the garlic."

Just then, the doorbell rings. Shay and Diego laugh.

"Just don't exhale," Diego says.

It's Detective Fusilli. He tries to keep this cordial expression on his face, especially when he sees that we're eating, but it is obvious that he is steamed, and I think I know the particular object of his rage. Still, he gives an appreciative glance at the pasta and grilled bread with olive oil and garlic, the green salad gleaming with dressing. Suddenly, he looks hungry as well as tired and angry.

Shay pushes away her glass of wine nervously, as if Joe Fusilli was doing a spot check for Mothers Who Drink and Cook. "Can I help you, Detective?" she asks.

Detective Fusilli tears his gaze away from the pasta. I exchange a glance with Diego. It's the first time we've found something funny at the same moment. I wonder if Joe Fusilli is just dying to take off his jacket, hang up his gun (I can't see it, but I know it's there), and sit down for a bowl of linguine.

"I need to talk to you and your daughter," he says.

"I'm her niece," I correct quickly, before Shay has a chance to.

"My sister died a year and a half ago," Shay explains.

"I'm sorry." For a moment, Detective Fusilli looks human. But then something else kicks in behind his eyes, and he gives me a quick glance. It's only a flicker, but I'm beginning to read Joe Fusilli like *Green Eggs and Ham.* He's thinking, *motherless girl, orphan, possible emotional problems, stirring up trouble for attention.*

Shay covers the bowl with a plate, and we all troop out to the living room. Everyone sits except for Diego, who lurks in the doorway. It's still light out, the long light of a Northwest summer. The sun shines right in my face, and I consider changing my seat, but I wonder if that would make me look guilty.

"Are you aware that your niece went to the Carbonel house this afternoon and told them she had a vision about their daughter?" Detective Fusilli asks Shay.

Surprised, Shay looks at me.

"I drove her over," Diego says. "I thought it might help."

Shay looks at Diego now. She turns back to Detective Fusilli and doesn't say anything.

He leans forward. "She told them Emily was still alive. Can you imagine how much damage she did to those people?"

"By giving them hope?" Shay asks.

He leans back again, but he keeps his eyes on Shay. "What if it's false hope?"

"What difference does it make?" Shay asks, surprising me.

That takes Joe Fusilli aback. I can see it. He turns the question over in his mind.

"Well, let me start with this," he says. "Your niece here —"

"Her name is Gracie," Shay interrupts tartly. Her skin is flushed.

"— told them that she saw a waterfall. Mrs. Carbonel wants us to check out every single waterfall in Washington State because your niece — Gracie here, saw one in a vision. Don't you think that might be an incredible waste of resources? And don't you think, if we don't do what Mrs. Carbonel wants, she's going to think that no matter what we do, it isn't enough?"

"Hey," Diego says, "what if Gracie's vision is true?"

The detective sighs. He runs a hand through his hair. There is a bottle of antacids in his car, and he wishes it was in his pocket.

"Too much TV," he says tiredly. "Too many movies. People think that psychics help cops out. They think psychics can find people. It just doesn't happen that way."

"Cops do use psychics," I say. "I read about it."

They all look at me, as if they're startled I can speak.

Joe Fusilli's gaze is especially intent. It's like he's a tracking device, and now he's totally focused on me. His voice is soft. "So you read about it, Gracie?" he asks, and I realize that I've made a big mistake. *So that's where you got the idea to make things up?* I can't read his mind, but I know what he's thinking.

I feel my face flush, and I hate myself for showing him he's caught me off guard. "It happens," I say. "It *has* happened. I've read the cases."

"So you thought you could help us with Emily," Joe Fusilli says. "Let me go over what you told Mrs. Carbonel." He reaches into his breast pocket and takes out a small pad. He starts to read. "Gracie was transported over water on a boat."

I realize this is a show he's putting on. He's deliberately trying to embarrass me. We live on an island. Lots of people have boats. There is a bridge about fifty miles north of us, but the ferry gets more traffic, because it's the quickest way to Seattle. There is a better than fifty-fifty chance that Emily left by boat.

"Was it the ferry?" he asks me.

I shake my head. "It was some kind of powerboat. It was going very fast."

"Ah, a new detail." He makes a show of writing this down. "And you say Emily was with someone she trusts. How do you know that?"

"She was laughing."

"You saw that in your vision?"

I nod.

"Why was she laughing?"

"Because the boat was going fast, and she was having fun." That was very clear to me. Emily had felt free.

"Did you see her by the waterfall?"

"No. I just saw a waterfall. But it was weird." I'm trying to remember now. I know the detective isn't really interested in this. But I know something wasn't right about that waterfall. I just can't figure out what.

"Weird?"

"No sound," I say. "But it wasn't just that. I don't know," I say finally, unable to put it into words.

"All right, then, Gracie. I have copied down everything you remember. Is that all you remember?"

"Yes," I say, because there is no way I'm telling him any more than I have already. He's going to walk out the door, tear out the page he's written on, ball it up, and throw it on the floor of his car, along with what I'm sure are crumpled fast-food wrappers, a sweaty T-shirt, and crumpled cans of diet Sprite.

And because I want to get back at him, I say, "I'm sorry about your mother."

He goes still. "My mother."

"She has Alzheimer's. You're always able to help people. And now you can't. When it's most important."

Everybody kind of freezes for a minute. Detective Fusilli's face doesn't reveal what he's thinking, but he's furious and not happy to find himself just a little confused. He takes a breath and casually puts his pad back into his pocket.

"I was the chairman of the annual Alzheimer's fundraiser. It was in the paper last month."

"I don't read the paper."

He dismisses this. He had been off his stride for a moment, but now he's figured out an explanation, so he can dismiss what I say. He leans forward, resting his elbows on his knees. "Tell me something, Gracie. You say that Emily was with someone she trusts. You know this because of your vision."

I wait.

"Is that the only reason you know it, Gracie?" Joe Fusilli asks. His voice is very soft now.

"Yes," I say. "I told you that already."

"Are you sure?"

"Do you want to hear it three times?"

"Because if there's something you have to tell me, now would be a good time. A very good time." There is something threatening in his voice now. He's leaning on me, hard.

Shay suddenly bounds to her feet. "That's enough," she says. "You are harassing my niece."

"I just want the truth," Detective Fusilli says, his eyes still on me. "There's a young girl out there we're trying to find."

"Gracie's a minor, I'm her guardian," Shay says, not giving an inch. "So get out."

Joe Fusilli gives Shay a cool look, as though her anger doesn't affect him in the least. "I was just leaving," he says, standing up. "You might want to have a talk with your niece, Ms. Kenzie. If she knows more than she's telling —"

"She told you she doesn't!" Shay snaps, her eyes blazing.

"Let's keep our focus here," Joe Fusilli says. "Our focus is Emily."

Now Shay *really* gets angry. Her hands actually curl into fists, and for a moment I'm afraid she'll haul off and land one on the detective.

Instead she whirls around and heads for the front door. She opens it with such force it bangs against the wall. "I haven't forgotten about Emily for one *second* since this happened," she spits out. "Her parents are close friends of mine. I've known her since she was born. We are all living with this, Detective. We are all in our separate hells about it." Suddenly, it's like Shay's throat closes over the words. "Now get out of my house."

He looks at Shay for a moment, then walks out the door. Shay closes the door very gently. She composes herself, still facing the door, before she turns back to us.

There is a long pause. Then Diego speaks.

"Detective Pasta sure knows how to push your buttons," he says.

We hear Detective Pasta start his car and take off.

He thinks I know something more than I'm telling. And I do. I'm just not sure what it is, and he is not the person I can tell it to. Nobody is. I'm alone. This is not in any way news to me.

But now being alone in the world has a new weight. Somebody has to find Emily Carbonel.

That someone, I now realize, is me.

NINE

From the very first week I arrived, Shay had declared that Sunday was Field Trip Day. *It will be fun!* she said. *Gracie needs to have a sense of place! And it will give us a chance to explore!*

Subtext: *I Don't Care If You Have Plans, Diego, We Are Going To Bond With Gracie Even If It Kills Us.*

So we got in the car, and I wore my headphones, and after trying to get me to "contribute," Shay pretty much left me alone, and she and Diego talked in the front seat. I saw Seattle, I saw Bainbridge Island, I saw Mount Rainier, I saw La Conner, I saw Desolation Pass. I was one big, walking Pacific Northwest bumper sticker.

Today, the sightseeing has to fit around our mission. Shay wants to drop by Rocky's studio in Seattle and leave a food basket. She's baked bread, made a marinara sauce, put some pasta and cheeses and a salami in there. As if Rocky couldn't walk out his front door and buy all those things in two blocks. As if eating pasta would make him forget that his daughter is missing.

And, not incidentally, as if I want to see him again. I am currently far from his favorite person.

"I spoke to Rocky," Shay says, not looking at me as she packs the basket. "He's sorry about the way he reacted. He knows you're just trying to help. We're all doing the best we can."

She closes the basket and sighs. "I know bringing food won't make a difference. I just have to do something."

In other words, I want to say, *you're doing this for you, not him.*

I remember casseroles rolling through the door after Mom's funeral. Little cards would be pinned to them. *Bake at 375° for one hour.* As if macaroni and cheese could matter. Could make a difference. As if eating food wasn't some gray experience, a forkful here and there of something you don't even taste, because someone says, "You have to eat," so you eat, just so they'll stop talking to you.

Thinking of that makes my throat feel tight, so I pull my headphones on and go out to wait in the car.

We take the ferry over to the mainland, and Shay drives to Rocky's studio, a restored boat factory on Lake Union. I know that Rocky has moved into his studio until he can find a house. Emily used to come here for weekends. She'd said the place spooked her because it got so empty at night. The neighborhood is still partly industrial.

Shay squeezes her old Saab into a space behind

a boat trailer, and we all pile out, Shay grabbing the food basket. She knocks on the door of the studio. After about a full minute, we hear footsteps clomping on the floor. The door opens, and a guy a little older than Diego stands there, squinting at us. He's slim, with sleek dark hair to his shoulders and eyes like chips of gray ice. His jeans are spotted with paint and his blue plaid flannel shirt has been laundered so many times it's almost white. Underneath it, he wears a T-shirt that was once black and is now almost green. Together with those pale gray eyes, he certainly looks well-washed.

"Hi, Zed," Shay says. "How're you doing?"

"What's up?" Which is not really an answer, I note. This guy is too cool to even say, "Okay."

"Is . . ."

"He went for a walk up at Green Lake. I kicked him out, actually. He needed some air, man."

Shay nods sympathetically.

"He's got his cell on, though, if you —"

"It's okay," Shay says. "I just wanted to drop this off." She points to the basket and shrugs. "Just some food. Do you know my son, Diego? And this is my niece, Gracie."

Zed's pale eyes flick over me. It is the shortest of glances, but I feel my face heat up. He doesn't say hello, or even nod, just stands aside to let us in. Thanks for making an effort, Mr. Handsome.

As I brush by him, I pick up an emotion.

Worry. Worry about Rocky? Worry about something else? I don't know, but I know he chews on that worry like a cow on grass.

We walk into a sort of living room, with a cushy couch and a long table with some of Rocky's glass pieces on it. They're big vases shaped like chrome kitchen garbage cans. There's even black shiny stuff that's supposed to look like a Hefty bag rolled over the top of the rim. I'd seen Rocky's work in Emily's house — well, I passed by some vases and things on the way to the refrigerator — but these were big and different and kind of cool.

Zed passes them by without a look and pushes open another door that leads into the studio area. It's just one huge room. One wall is full of books on metal shelves. Long tables are in the middle of the open space, with paper and pastel crayons scattered on them. Big drawings of vases and vessels are drawn with huge loopy lines. The drawings are in black and white and blocks of bright color are in the margins, as if Rocky is trying to figure out what color they should be.

A couch that matches the one in the other room is against one wall and has sheets and a blanket neatly draped over one arm. There's a wooden screen in the other corner with a map painted on it. I realize that it's a cartoony version of Beewick Island. Behind the screen is a rolled-up futon and a small table. Wooden cubes with clothes in them are stacked next to the bed, and I recognize some T-shirts of Emily's. So that's where she slept when she visited. Some dried lavender is stuck in a pretty yellow vase on the table. That makes me feel sad, because I see that Rocky had tried to make the place sort of homey for Emily, and I know it hadn't worked.

"Are you blowing today?" Shay asks.

Zed nods. "Going to try, anyway. Work might help."

Shay puts the basket down. "How is Rocky doing?"

Zed leans over and shuts the lid of the computer. "I don't think he sleeps."

I drift away, over toward Emily's corner. Shay is moving over to look at a table with some sketches. She is talking to Zed about Rocky, who, according to Zed, is a "freaking mess."

I see a T-shirt, neatly folded in one of the cubes, and pick it up. It's from the computer camp that Emily never got a chance to go to this summer. She was so proud of getting into that camp. It's a bright red shirt — not Emily's best color, but she wore it a lot at the end of school. Then she stopped wearing it.

The room fades suddenly, the gray walls rushing toward me like a waterfall. Then the water is like a wave, a gentle wave splashing against a beach full of pebbles. The pebbles are grayish, opalescent.

Then the gray bleaches to white, and I'm looking at a bed. Light sweeps across it, and then darkness comes again.

I'm standing in a doorway, looking down at Emily on a white bed.

I'm angry at her.

I'm angry at all of them.

It's all their fault, and they won't try hard enough, and it's all about that, isn't it?

If only they would listen to me. If only they would see that we have to share. That we have to love one another.

If only they could see that.

How much harder can I try?

They make me sick, they make me so mad . . .

The walls move back again, and I'm in the studio. The fear starts from the ground up. I feel it surge through me and I want to scream. I want to run outside and gulp air. My mouth tastes like greasy coins.

I've been in his head.

I've been in the kidnapper's head.

I've seen through his eyes. I've felt what he's been feeling.

He's on the edge of something. It's like he's holding back a great torrent of black emotion, holding it back with the fraying ribbons of his control.

And Emily was there. I saw Emily.

But this time, I didn't really register her. I was too overwhelmed by the thoughts. Emily hadn't been a real person to me.

Because I was looking at her through his eyes.

I sink onto the futon.

She's not a real person to him.

It makes me feel sick to my stomach.

She existed *for* him. She wasn't *Emily* to him.

How could someone look at someone else and be so detached, so . . . *wrong*?

I realize that I've crushed Emily's T-shirt in my hands. They feel stiff as I try to smooth out the shirt. Something tells me to act normal, not to call attention to what just happened.

I get up and walk toward Diego, who has wandered over to another door. I just need somewhere to move. As he opens the door, I see something. Flames.

I shake my head. Is that something I see, or something I imagine?

I walk quickly to the doorway, my heart pounding now. I stand in the doorway and see the ovens. The opening of the oven is square, and flames are shooting up, burning hot and orange.

A white square with flames shooting out . . .

"What is it?" I ask.

Diego turns slightly. "It's called the glory hole. It's where the glass is kept hot before it's shaped."

I'm so confused I can't think clearly. There's too much information flooding me at once. I can't pick up one single thread. When I hear Shay's voice behind me, I jump.

"Time to go," she says.

I turn automatically. We walk toward the door.

"I'll stop by the Harborside soon," Shay says to Zed. "You working tonight?"

"No, next weekend." Zed nods for a good-bye. His eyes meet mine for a brief second. I don't know whether I'm chilled or attracted. There is so much that is wrong here that I can't pick out what is important, what I need to know.

The door closes behind us. I take a breath of fresh air, but it feels thick and humid and doesn't help to clear my head.

The beach. The light, then darkness. The man standing in the doorway. The flames.

What does it have to do with Emily? Are they clues I can follow? How can I find Emily based on flashes that come in bursts of light and then go before I really *see* anything?

I'm so balled up with frustration I want to howl and kick the car door.

I am sick inside, and afraid.

What I really want to do is walk away. Walk away from all of them, from all of this.

But I'm trapped, and I know it. I push away the

panic, grind it down with my foot. I try to hone in on the first thing I can. Zed's worry. What was it about?

"The Harborside?" I ask as we walk toward the car.

"Zed's father owns a restaurant on Beewick Island. Zed cooks there on the weekends. He stays in a fishing shack near the place," Shay explains. "Zed became a gaffer for Rocky just recently, when he got out of college. He also happens to be the fastest oyster-shucker on Beewick Island. Which means he's probably the fastest oyster shucker just about anywhere."

Shay opens the car doors, and we pile in.

Oysters.

Those weren't beach pebbles I saw, they were *shells*. Oyster shells.

I look down and realize that Emily's shirt is still bunched up in my hand. I put it down carefully and buckle my seat belt. "Where's the Harborside?"

"In Greystone Harbor," Shay says, pulling out of the parking spot.

Greystone Harbor is the next town over on Beewick. It's where the tourists go. The town is pretty, white houses and flowering bushes, all built around a horseshoe-shaped cove. Very postcardy. There's even a lighthouse.

Light sweeping, then darkness. Was that a lighthouse in my vision?

Let's get ice cream, Emily had said. The ice cream place is in Greystone Harbor.

A long, hot walk on the hottest day of the year. She couldn't have wanted ice cream *that* badly.

I remember Zed's silver eyes, the way he looked at me. Had Emily ever mentioned him?

I remember asking her how her weekends were in Seattle. She'd said they were grim. She said Rocky trying to please her made her feel strange. Usually, the weekend would disintegrate somehow, and Emily would suggest that Rocky go to work. She liked to watch him blow glass.

And she'd said, *But the sightseeing is pretty fine, if you know what I mean.*

Clueless me thought she was talking about . . . sightseeing. But I think back on the way she said it now, and I realize what she meant. She'd been talking about Zed. Zed in his faded jeans, his tight T-shirts, his cool, silvery eyes.

Zed with the worry inside that doesn't go away, no matter how much he tries to bury it.

TEN

Shay takes us out for an afternoon of fun, she says. We watch them throw salmon for the tourists in the Public Market. We have an early dinner at Etta's, and then we go to a big, old bookstore in Pioneer Square, which Shay calls a Seattle landmark. I lose Shay in Cooking and Diego in History.

I wish I could lose myself.

It's like this thing with Emily has cracked me open, and I don't want to say *like a nut*. But suddenly, it's like I can read what other people are feeling. Not Shay, and not Diego. Not everyone I see. But sometimes, a wave hits me, and I *know*.

I know that the fat man in Travel is worried about his daughter's marriage.

The woman in head-to-toe Gore-Tex just threw up in the bathroom. She's pregnant.

It's a girl, I want to tell her. *Don't worry so much.*

The man in the green shirt taking down a book in Fiction wonders why books can't save him from falling in love with women who hurt him.

The woman with the long silver ponytail has a doctor's appointment tomorrow. She's worrying about cancer as she chooses a book called *Living Simply in an Age of Stress.*

You're okay, I want to tell her.

But what good would it do? She'd think I was just another passing lunatic.

Emily isn't okay.

I've got to screen everything else out. I've got to figure it out, I've got to decipher it.

I've got to break it down.

I go downstairs to this little café they have. They're out of soda, and the girl behind the counter suggests coffee.

"I don't drink coffee," I say, which I realize is enough to get me deported from the city of Seattle.

"We have juice," the girl behind the counter says. She has a pierced eyebrow and a seriously punked-out haircut. Her gaze is somewhere between hostile and bored. She hates her job and pretty much hates her life, but I'm relieved that I get no insight, no flash into why.

"I don't like juice," I say.

She shrugs. I finally ask for tea, which I don't really want. I find a table and start dunking the teabag like I'm trying to wash it clean.

Forget about the visions, I tell myself. What else did you see?

Detective Fusilli had asked me if Emily had a crush, and I'd said that Emily never talked about boys. I thought I'd been telling the truth. But what if she'd been *trying* to talk to me about a crush, only I was too dense, too locked in my own head, too busy trying to hear music that I wanted always, always playing? I wanted the music to block out everything in my head, and it wound up blocking someone talking just a couple of feet away.

I remember Zed closing the laptop as Shay moved toward the table. Had he been hiding something? How could I get back into the studio and find out? I couldn't drive, which was a serious handicap. I discovered something essential: Detectives need cars.

Maybe I could talk Shay into going back so that she could see Rocky. Why was she taking him food, anyway? Why wasn't she taking food to Mrs. Carbonel? Did Shay have a crush on Rocky? Was she using this as an opportunity to move in on him? That would be totally snaky of her, but I really don't know how Shay operates in her love life. All I know is that for an overweight middle-aged woman, she has plenty of dates. You'd think on an island you'd run out of men at some point.

Maybe I'm wrong. Maybe Shay and Rocky are *already* involved. Maybe Shay is the reason the Carbonel marriage broke up. I try to think back about that night we went over there. Mrs. Carbonel hadn't even said hello to Shay.

Shay plunks down a bag of books on the table,

making me jump. She points to the tea with her chin.

"I didn't know you liked tea."

I push the tea away. She sits down. I look at her sandaled feet, then look away. Shay has feet like a hobbit. Her toes are chunky and round. You'd think that if you had toes like that, you wouldn't want to call attention to them. You'd be too embarrassed to get pedicures. Not Shay. Her toenails are bright red.

"Don't you want to buy a book or two? I'm treating," Shay says.

I shake my head.

Shay looks distracted. She lifts her hair off her neck and lets it fall again. Her hair is thick like my mom's, but it's brown, not blond. Not that my mom's was natural. Mom used to call me her "tell," which meant that because I have brown hair, everyone would know her blond hair was fake. She used to ruffle my hair when she said it; she really didn't care, she was making a joke. I feel anger grip me in a fist and squeeze. Shay's feet, her hair, annoy me. Her breath, the fact that she's breathing. The fact that I'm sitting here, in a strange place, with a stranger, miles away from what I know. What I've loved.

"Are you after Rocky?" I ask her.

Shay looks confused for a minute. "Am I . . ."

"Are you trying to move in on him?" I ask. "Is that why you're bringing him food?"

Knowledge floods Shay's eyes. I see it happen, filling her brain as the blush fills her cheeks. So it's true.

"That's a horrible thing to say," she says.

She is furious. I've never seen her angry, at least at me. Only at Detective Fusilli, or at a driver going too fast on a country road.

"You think I'm using Emily's disappearance to spice up my *love life*?" she asks. Her green eyes are intense, watching my face.

I shrug. I press my finger on the teabag on the table and watch the brown stain spread out.

Shay stands up. "I'll meet you at the car," she says.

I sit there for a few minutes. I'm not feeling too great about myself. I tell myself that detectives have to ask questions that people don't want to answer, but deep down, I know something that I'm afraid to admit. I *enjoyed* asking the question.

Finally, I stand up. Diego is coming down the stairs to get me. He waits while I wipe up the tea and throw the napkin and cup away. We walk to the car without saying anything. I can tell he knows Shay is upset, but I'm not sure if he knows why.

Shay is sitting in the driver's seat. "I hope we don't hit traffic," she says in a neutral voice. "There's a Mariners game letting out."

We do hit traffic, but I think she's relieved, because she gets to concentrate on driving. I want to say something, but I don't know what. So I start thinking about how to investigate Zed. It's up to me, and I know it. If I go to the police and babble about oyster shells and feelings, they'll laugh me out the door.

Shay had said that he stays in a shack on the beach. If I could get inside, maybe I could find something.

Or maybe *Emily* could be inside. Maybe Zed got her to go away with him, but then she changed her mind. Maybe he's keeping her there, and that's what I saw in the vision.

"Why don't we stop for ice cream on the way home?" I suggest.

Diego turns from the front seat and looks at me, surprised. Shay glances in the rearview mirror. It's the first time I have ever suggested prolonging an outing. It could be the first time I've suggested doing *anything* together.

"How about that place in Greystone Harbor?" I say.

I see how Shay's face relaxes. I realize that she thinks that this is my way to apologize. I'm embarrassed. I should have thought of it as an apology. Instead, it's just a ruse. But at least it gets me somewhere closer to Emily.

ELEVEN

Diego gets vanilla, which is weird, because I'd never peg him for a vanilla person. Shay gets chocolate, which is not a surprise. I get toasted coconut. Diego knows the pretty girl who serves the ice cream, of course, since he knows every pretty girl on Beewick. So he hangs out at the counter, licking his cone, while she giggles and pretends to fill napkin containers.

I've got news for Diego. She likes him, but she's using him. She's overdoing the giggles, hoping her boyfriend comes early to pick her up so she can make him jealous.

Shay and I head for a table. The silence is awkward, at least for me. Shay licks her cone and looks out the window. The sun has already set, and we're getting the last of the light. Across the street from us are the restaurants and shops at the harbor's edge. They're built up on a kind of pier over the beach. I can see the lights of the Harborside, which looks like the kind of place Bluebeard's pirates might hang out in. Creaky wood siding and lanterns outside casting dim pools of light into the dusk. Fishnets hung on the siding. All for the benefit of the tourists.

Emily, where are you?

If I can pick up the feelings of strangers, why can't I feel you here?

I saw the house in the dunes as we drove down the harbor road, but I can't see it from here, it's around the point. It looks like an old fisherman's shack. It couldn't be more than one room.

"I'm sorry I got up and left," Shay says finally. She still looks out at the fading light. "I was just so *mad*."

"I was just asking," I said.

"But you thought it might be true."

"I don't know you," I blurt out.

She looks at me.

"I don't know what kind of person you are," I say. "So I don't know if you would be the kind of person to have a crush on Rocky, and bring him food, and think that comforting him would . . ."

Shay's mouth twists. "Get me what I want?"

I don't answer.

"Okay," Shay says. "I'm not that kind of person, first of all. I'm more the kind of person that does dumb things like bring people food when I don't know what else to do. I was a friend of both Rocky and Laura when they were together and I'm still a friend. Not a close friend, but a friend. I'm not attracted to Rocky. He's a piece of work, if you want to know the truth. I like him, I just wouldn't want to be involved with him. Okay?"

"Okay," I say. The ice cream is melting on my hand, and I lick it off.

Shay takes a breath. "What hurts me," she says in a slow, careful voice, "is that I felt like you *wanted* it to be true."

I think about this and realize that she's right.

Mostly, I don't want to be having this conversation. The light is going, and I need to find a way to leave and prowl around that shack. But it would be too weird to get up now.

"I don't want to get all psychodrama-ish about this," Shay says, "but has it occurred to you that resenting me for not being your mother is a waste of time?"

"You're just so not like her," I say. "Like you're from a different family."

She grins and takes a lick of her cone. "True. We were always opposites. Your mom knew what she wanted to do, and she did it. She was on the debating team in, like, fifth grade. She always knew she wanted to be a lawyer. Graduated from college right before her twentieth birthday. I was on the five-year plan. Me, I just wanted to sleep at the beach, tool around in a boat, go crabbing. It wasn't until I was thirty that I realized that loving water could be a profession. That's when I went back to school to study wetlands. You should have seen your grand-parents. They turned cartwheels. They thought I'd end up, I don't know," and Shay waves her ice-cream cone to take in the shop, "dishing up ice cream on the boardwalk in New Jersey."

Shay crunches on her cone. "Carrie was a force of nature, that's for sure. She never let up; she never gave in. You should have seen her on the swim team in high school." She smiles. "You should have seen that water churn."

I didn't ask for a eulogy, I want to say. But I'd said enough mean things to Shay already that day.

"Being opposites doesn't mean you can't be close," Shay says. "Look at you and Emily."

Everyone thinks I'm Emily's best friend. The truth is, I care about her more now that she's missing.

Guilt may be a pathetic propellant, but it works. I want so badly to get up from the table that my knees are shaking.

"One time, your mom and I decided to become blonds together," Shay says, a smile on her face. "We had to hide the box from your grandmother. Carrie went first. She —"

But I switch her off. I don't want to hear Shay's memories. I can't handle the memories I have. I sure don't need anybody else's.

I don't care how weird it looks. I have to get out of here.

I stand up. "I need to take a walk."

Shay's face flushes. She's not angry. She's kicking herself because she thinks she's handled this badly. "I'll come with you," she says, starting to stand.

"That's okay. I just want some air."

I leave her there, her chocolate ice cream dripping down her hand, staring after me.

The air is cooler off the water. I walk down the street, away from Shay's sight line. I'll have to double back, go under the piers so she won't see me. I don't have much time. As soon as I'm out of sight, I start to jog.

There's no moon tonight. The lights from the restaurants don't penetrate the dark of the beach. The sand sucks at my shoes. I begin to feel something skitter along my skin, ruffle the hairs on my arms. If I'm right, what will I find in that shack?

Emily wasn't moving in my vision. She was so still.

For the first time, it occurs to me that Emily could be dead.

TWELVE

Dark . . . light. Dark . . . light. The beam from the lighthouse sweeps the harbor. As I walk, it sweeps over me. Every few seconds, I feel exposed, even though I'm walking up near the dunes and there are scrubby pine trees here for cover.

There are curtains at the windows of the shack, and no light seeps out through the cracks. I leave the shelter of the trees and walk toward it.

When I'm up against the wall of the shack, I try to peer into the window. Not only does it have a curtain, the windowpane is frosted with salt. I can't see a thing.

As I try to peer in, the window moves slightly, and I realize that it's hinged on top. All I have to do is pull the bottom out, which I do. I look around. The beach is deserted. I pull the window open and put in my foot.

It's hard to climb in a window, especially when you're so scared your muscles aren't working right. I manage to slither inside, still holding the window out. I let it fall behind me.

It's too dark inside to see more than shapes at first.

"Emily?" I whisper. My heart is booming, rushing in my ears.

I am able to make out now that the shape in the corner is a bed. There's one chair, one small table. A few books are stacked on the floor. There's no sink, no bathroom. Just a bottle of water by the bed.

No Emily.

My heart is beginning to slow down. I start to explore what little there is. I go through his books, which are mostly art books, with some fiction by young male writers thrown in.

I flip through the books, and a piece of paper flies out of one and slowly wafts downward, where it hits my shoe. I pick it up.

It's a copy of an e-mail.

To: glazboy
From: eminel
Subject: book
Z,
This was life-changing. Which means you are, too, I guess. Too much pressure? Sorry. Only I'm not.
E

Emily.

I stare at the paper, knowing what it means. It means Emily and Zed had something going on.

Then something touches my ankle.

I scream. I leap off the bed and land on the other side of the room. I'm backing up toward the window when a gray cat pokes its nose out from under the bed.

I put my hand on my chest and beg my heart not to explode. I bend down and look. The cat's yellow eyes shine out at me.

"Hey, cat," I say softly.

She stretches, then steps out daintily a few inches, just like cats do, telling me that she's not in the mood to socialize, but she'll endure me.

I tuck the note into my pocket and replace the book on the floor with the others. That's when I notice a small dish of dry cat food in the corner, along with a bowl of water. If I'd seen it on my first inspection of the room, I would have spared myself a major heart attack.

As I stare at the cat food, it occurs to me that if there is a cat here, with a full bowl of food, it stands to reason that the cat's owner is currently in residence, and not an hour away in Seattle. He's here, now. Somewhere.

Crunch, crunch.

It isn't the cat, munching on her kibble. It's footsteps. On the beach. Coming closer.

I peer out the window. It's Zed.

I jump back, even though I know he can't see me. There is nowhere to hide in a one-room shack.

The door and only window face the beach, where Zed is. There is nowhere to go.

I touch the paper in my pocket. I have proof that Zed had some kind of relationship with Emily, something he'd hidden from Rocky. That doesn't make him guilty, but it does make him a suspect. Which means he could be dangerous.

I look outside again and see Zed trudging toward the shack. And then suddenly the moon comes out, and I see that it's raining.

Zed is carrying a body in his arms.

A girl.

She's wearing a nightgown, and the rain is starting to plaster it to her legs.

Her head lolls back, and he tries to keep it up.

I feel cold, frozen to the bone.

I know that the girl is dead.

Then something happens — I blink, or the world shifts and turns a fraction — and it's Zed again, just trudging across the sand, tired after a long day.

It was a vision. Of the future? Of the past?

Of Zed carrying Emily.

And Emily is dead.

But had it really been Zed? Had it been Emily?

Now I'm not so sure.

Enough! I want to scream. I can't figure it out, I can never figure it out, and yet the visions keep on coming. And Emily is getting farther and farther away.

I won't be able to find her, I won't be able to interpret what I see, and it will be too late, and all my life I will know that I could have saved her, could have done something, only I was *just too stupid to figure it out*!

I am shivering now, shaking. The cat jumps back down and scoots under the bed.

I have a more immediate problem. Zed is going to arrive any minute and find me.

I hear someone calling Zed's name. Even through the closed window, I can hear it.

I see Diego running down the beach, running fast, calling as he runs. Zed stops and waits for Diego to catch up. Diego says something I can't hear, waving his arms, pointing. Zed shrugs. Diego talks again.

Zed has turned his back to the shack to talk to Diego. I push the window open and climb out, managing to do it without falling or making noise. My legs are shaking as I run around the back of the shack and into the dark pools of shadows from the pines. I can't get to the road from here; I have to walk down to the beach and retrace my steps. I start to walk along the dunes, hoping that it's too dark for Diego and Zed to see me.

I could wait in the shelter of the pines, but I have a feeling that if I'm gone much longer, Shay will be calling Detective Pasta. I walk quickly across the pebbly part of the dunes. It's really awkward trying to walk quickly and quietly on rocky sand.

"Gracie!"

I want to keep walking, but I turn. Diego is waving at me, with a big, stupid grin on his face. I've never seen him direct that grin toward me before.

Zed looks at me. It's too dark to see what his expression is. I walk slowly toward them, wishing with every step I was walking the other way.

"Hi," I chirp. Once, a mouse got in our kitchen and climbed into the trash can and started squeaking. Our dog, Pooka, went over, jumped up on the can, looked in, and barked at the mouse, which promptly dropped dead of a heart attack.

I feel like that mouse. My teeth are chattering, and I grind them into a smile. I feel like I might pass out. I can't look at Zed. I can only remember him walking with a dead girl in his arms. I can only push back the fear that it was Emily.

"Where've you been?" Diego asks amiably. "Shay is about to call in the FBI."

"I told her I was going for a walk," I say.

"Did you get lost?"

I realize he's given me a great save. "Just a little."

He reaches out and knocks my head with his knuckles. "D'oh." What is this big-brother act he's putting on?

"Thanks, anyway," he says to Zed. "I guess we found her without looking."

Zed's eyes are the color of the moon, and just as remote. "See you, then."

"See ya," Diego calls, already walking without waiting for me to catch up. Which I do. I run. I'm glad of the company, even if it's Diego.

For a while I just hear the soft slap of the water and the scrunch of our footsteps in the damp sand.

Then Diego explodes. His voice hisses like the waves. "Are you nuts? Who do you think you are, Nancy Drew?"

"I don't know what you're . . ."

"I saw you come out of Zed's shack, Gracie, okay? I had a feeling that's where you were heading. If you want to be a detective, get a new face. I saw how you were looking at Zed at Rocky's studio. At first, I thought you were into him, but then I realized you were after him. It's insane to investigate on your own. Whoever took Emily . . . she could . . . *anything* could have happened, okay?"

It's the longest speech Diego has ever given. He's really steamed.

We're under the piers now. It's a creepy place to be, in the dark. I look over my shoulder. The beach is deserted. No one is behind us. But the pillars make me nervous. There are so many places to hide.

"Could we just get to the sidewalk, please?" I ask.

He shoots me a look. Then he does a nice thing. He takes my hand and helps me up the slope of sand. He practically hauls me up onto the sidewalk.

"Explain," he says. "Here. Now. Shay can't see us. We have about thirty seconds before she freaks."

I hand him the note. He reads it.

"I found it in one of Zed's books," I say. "In the shack. Eminel is Emily's screen name."

Diego still stares at the note.

"When I was at Rocky's, I had a vision," I add. "I saw the light from a lighthouse sweeping over a bed. Emily was in the bed."

Diego looks up, out to the bay.

"The *lighthouse*," I say, even though I know he gets it. "And I saw oyster shells, lots of them. Shay said Zed was the champion oyster shucker. And I remembered something Emily said about weekends at Rocky's. I think she had a crush on Zed, and that note proves there was something between them."

"What else?" Diego asks.

I shake my head and turn away.

"Something spooked you, and it wasn't this note," Diego says. "You've got to trust someone, Gracie. Don't you see that this is too big for you to handle alone?"

Fury balls up like a fist inside my throat. Who does he think he is? I've handled the biggest thing in the *world* all alone. "I *am* alone," I say coldly.

"You're *not* alone," Diego says.

I don't say anything, I just look out at the water.

"When you first came to live with us, I was scared of you," Diego says. "Shay told me that you had some psychic experiences. I was scared that having some spook-doozy living with me would invade my privacy or something. Or that you'd see things about me, and they'd be all bad."

"It doesn't work that way," I say defensively. "I'm not an X-ray machine."

"I'm just saying, that's one reason why I didn't talk to you much."

"That's really stupid."

"Yeah, well, the other reason is that you're really a pain."

I laugh. I can't help it. Diego calling me spook-doozy helps somehow.

"So I just wanted to say that," he says.

"Okay."

"So tell me what else you saw."

I look at him and I see kindness in his face. He wants to help, and at least he doesn't think I'm crazy. "I saw a vision when Zed was crossing the beach," I tell him. "He was carrying a girl. A dead body. In the rain."

Diego sucks in his breath. "Was it Emily?"

"I *assumed* it was," I admit. "But I don't know for sure. I didn't see her face. I'm not even sure I saw his face."

"You know what we have to do, don't you?" Diego says.

I am already shaking my head, but I know I'll lose.

"The police have to know," Diego says. "That means we have to tell Shay first."

I just look at the sidewalk.

"She'll be cool," Diego assures me. "C'mon."

We start to walk back toward the ice cream parlor. I'm not too thrilled about the prospect of seeing Joe Fusilli again. But I'd much rather face the police than Shay.

THIRTEEN

One of Dr. Politsky's questions in therapy was "Can you name one thing that made you happy today?" I don't know why a question that always really bugged me won't get out of my head. So if I have to find a ray of sunshine in my current state, I'd have to say that after all, it is a relief to tell Shay that I've had a little episode of breaking and entering.

She doesn't yell. She doesn't move. She listens without talking, which is a highly unusual trait in a person, if you ask me. Diego is there for support. We sit in the living room, which feels weird and formal, because we're always in the kitchen. And after I am through and Shay looks sort of pale and shaken, she says we need to go to the police, which is exactly what Diego said would happen.

But she doesn't get up. She looks at me. "You have to trust me," she says. "You *have* to now, Gracie. It's too dangerous for you not to. You have to tell me what you know, and even what you suspect. Do you understand?"

I nod.

"I can't believe that Zed has anything to do with this," Shay says, shaking her head. "I've known him since he was a boy."

"You have to admit he's a weird guy, Mom," Diego says.

Shay looks reluctant to call anyone weird. "He's . . . different, okay," she says. "He's had it tough. His mother died when he was seven, and his dad works all night at the restaurant. He was raised by his dad's girlfriends. I can't imagine him kidnapping Emily, or being involved somehow." She shakes her head. "I hate going to the police, but we have to. This could be all my fault."

"What do you mean?" Diego asks, because Shay looks stricken. I see a vein throb in her forehead I'd never noticed before.

"Don't you remember?" Shay looks at Diego. "I'm the one who recommended that Rocky hire Zed in the first place."

We must have interrupted Detective Fusilli's late dinner, because there's a plastic bowl half-filled with salad on his desk. I see slivered chicken, I see noodles, I see red pepper, I see green beans. I thought police detectives were supposed to live on junk food.

He looks up and meets Shay's eyes. I feel the surge that he feels. I could have lived without knowing that Detective Joe Fusilli thinks that, if this were a different time and a different place, and he wasn't in charge of a missing-child case, he would like to experience what it would be like to really kiss Shay Kenzie.

You would never know it by his face, or his voice, or the way he looks at Shay, but the feeling is so strong I can pick it up like a megawatt radio station on a clear night. I also pick up that although he is glad to see Shay again, he is not particularly happy to see me.

We sit. Shay very calmly hands him the copy of the e-mail I found at Zed's shack, explaining that I, well, climbed inside.

"I can't take this," he says. "If it's evidence, it will be thrown out. I can't even read it," he says, reading it. He rubs his forehead.

"Did you know that Emily had a relationship with Zed Allen?" he asks.

"No," I say. "She never mentioned him. But thinking back, I remember something she said . . ."

"What?" Obviously, Detective Pasta is not one of those listeners who doesn't interrupt with questions.

"That she liked the sightseeing at her father's studio," I say. "I didn't pick it up at the time. I thought she was talking about boats. You can see boats from the windows," I add lamely. "But I think she was talking about Zed."

He taps the paper against the desk.

"He might still have the original on his computer," I say.

"I realize that," he says. "There's this thing I need called probable cause. Is there anything else you can give me to go on?" He speaks gently now. "I know it's not easy, Gracie. But just now, you told me something that's important, something you remembered and saw in a different light. Can you think of anything else like that?"

At first, I'm impatient with this question. I don't see how I can reinterpret something that didn't stick in my mind. I can't just pluck a sentence from my memory that Emily has said and shout, "That's it!"

But suddenly, I *do* remember something.

"The library," I blurt out. "Emily wanted to go to the library that day, the day she disappeared."

"Yes?" Detective Fusilli said.

"Emily wasn't a reader," I say.

"And? You think she was meeting someone?"

"I don't know," I say. "But the library has computers. If she wanted to send a message that she didn't want traced, she could go there."

Joe Fusilli nods slowly. I can see two things — frustration that he didn't think of this already, and relief that he has something to go on now.

I've given him a lead.

FOURTEEN

The police search Zed's computer. It's been wiped. There's no trace of e-mails or websites visited, not even buried in the hard drive. When they search the library computers, they find the same thing on two of them.

They want to talk to him, but Zed disappears.

The days pass, and they can't find him. Shay tells me all this after she gets home from work. Her head is in the refrigerator while she roots around for something to cook for dinner. I can see that she can't really focus on food, and for Shay, that's saying something. She takes out a lemon, a head of cabbage, and a cantaloupe.

She stares at them on the counter.

"There's always pizza," I say.

"I need to cook. Want to go to the grocery store?" she says.

I know she doesn't want to leave me alone. Diego didn't go to work today. He hung around the house, which he never does. We weeded the garden together, just because I couldn't stand to see him out there doing it by himself. I felt too guilty. We watched some lame afternoon TV. Diego chatted on the computer while I stared out the window and wished I'd have another vision that would clear everything up, even if I was too scared to try. Shay got home and released Diego from Gracie duty. He scooted out to see Marigold.

She tells me that they are checking out all the websites visited from the library on the afternoon Emily left, but so far it didn't sound like they'd found anything. The librarian remembered seeing her, but she doesn't remember if it was that day. If she had, she would have gone to the police already.

Another dead end. Another day.

But it's just us for dinner, and it will feel good to take a drive.

Shay grabs the keys, and I follow. We roll down all the windows and the blast of air is warm and smells like summer. I like the early evenings here best, when the sun is liquid and pours over the fields. The sky turns this incredible color, a blue so deep that it seems to vibrate, and the shadows of the pines are purple.

"The blue hour," Shay says. She smiles, loving it, too.

We drive to Greystone Harbor, where the good grocery store is. I trail along behind Shay as she buys salmon and greens for a salad. She picks up a tub of freshly baked cookies from the local bakery. When I used to go grocery shopping with Mom, she tossed things into the cart quickly, consulting her list. Shay never makes a list. She inhales, she peers, she talks to the fish man and the wine lady. I'm mildly bored, but the music is catchy. I hum along to "Secret Agent Man."

He's giving you a number, and taking away your name . . .

. . . taking away your name . . .

I go away and come back. I don't know how else to describe it. Something gray drops over me, like fuzz on a TV screen, and I hear Emily's voice in my head, and she says, "He took away our *names,*" and when I'm there next, I'm still standing next to the freezer section. My fingertips are against the glass. But that's not why I'm cold.

Fear again. I feel it. Multiplied.

Emily isn't the only one. There are others there with her.

Shay is wheeling the cart toward the cashier. I hurry toward her. I'm tired of visions. I'm tired of fear. I'm afraid of being here, in this grocery store, where visions can come as you're staring at packages of frozen French bread pizza.

I want to go home.

Shay pays for the groceries. She came for just a couple of things, but the cart is full. A man walks over to her with a smile and starts to talk to her. I slow down.

I walk up to them. Shay absentmindedly puts

her hand on my shoulder as the man finishes his sentence, something about a memo at work that everyone got that day, and Roger fouling things up again.

Shay introduces me to the co-worker, whose name I immediately forget. I need to be outside. I want to be home like a two-year-old.

"I'll load everything in the car," I say.

"Be right behind you," Shay says, handing me the keys. I can tell now that she really doesn't want to discuss Roger or the memo, but she's stuck.

I push the cart out into the parking lot. The lights are on now, and the blue has turned inky. The lot is almost empty now. I put the grocery bags in the trunk.

I hear the footsteps before I see anything, even a shadow. Someone is running, a whispery sound on the asphalt. I'm just turning to see, trying to get out of the way of the trunk lid, when something slams into my body. I start to fall, but I feel hands grab me.

I can't see behind me, but I feel his breath. He is very strong. The force of the slam carries us both over the side of the car and, before I know what is happening, he pulls me down the slope of the grass. We roll together, over the rocks and the roots, grunting, me trying to scream. But the breath has been knocked out of me, and we spill out together underneath the dark, dark trees.

No light overhead, no moon.

And yet I can see him.

I know him, his face over mine, his body pinning me down.

Zed.

FIFTEEN

"Just . . . don't . . . scream," he says. He puts his hand over my mouth.

I nod jerkily, quickly.

"What do they know?" he asks, his voice a hurtling ball of fury, fear. "What did you tell them?"

I think the word *who*, but I can't say it. My throat has closed from fear.

"The police!" he yells into my face. "I know you were in my place. Don't lie to me!"

The fear inside me has drained me of everything I have — bones, muscles, will. His eyes are chips of moon. I am falling into the earth underneath me.

I hear the noise of something falling down the slope, rocks sliding, someone breathing. Zed whips his head around, straining in the darkness.

She slams into him headfirst, using her body to push him off me. I hear the thud of their bodies connecting.

"Get off her!" Shay shouts, and she pummels him until he rolls away. She kneels next to me and scoops me up and holds me. Her eyes are wide and frightened. "Gracie?"

I nod to show I'm okay. She turns, holding me against her and faces off against Zed. But he doesn't give her time to say or do anything. He's scrambling up the hill on all fours, grabbing chunks of dirt and rocks and sliding down, then gaining a few inches. Finally, he finds his feet and scoots the rest of the way, over the lip of the hill, and we lose sight of him. Then I realize that the high-pitched noise I've been hearing hasn't been my breathing. Sirens.

Shay is hugging me, rocking me. In the past, when she hugged me, I was repulsed by her softness. This time, all I feel is muscle. I lean into it, glad of it.

"I'm sorry, I'm sorry," she is saying. "I never should have let you go into the parking lot like that. Alone."

I find my voice at last. "It's okay," I croak.

"I'm sorry," she keeps saying, crying into my hair.

We hear the sounds above in the parking lot but can't see it. The squeal of tires. Someone yelling.

"Nice and easy!" someone shouts.

Shay looks up. "They got him," she whispers.

My legs are shaking badly, but Shay helps me, and we get up the hill and back to the parking lot. Zed is being frisked, his legs out, his hands on the police car. Under the streetlights and next to the uniformed cops, he just looks like a skinny kid in a torn T-shirt and dirty jeans.

Joe Fusilli is there, in another car. He sees us and hurries toward us. "What are you doing here?" he bellows.

Shay's worry for me now moves into a channel she can groove on — irritation at Detective Pasta. She waves at the grocery store. "Maybe, like, buying food? Until Zed grabbed Gracie and tried to kidnap her! Where were you?"

Joe's gaze makes that abrupt turn into concentration, and he focuses on me. "What happened?"

I explain how I was putting the groceries in the car, and Zed tackled me. Then Shay says that she came out and saw the trunk open and got scared, and started to look around. She saw me down in the grove of trees and came after Zed.

"We had a report he was down in Greystone Harbor," Joe Fusilli says. "We were cruising and just happened to spot him. Can you come down to the station? Now we have him for attempted kidnapping and assault, too. Come on, I'll drive."

"I have my car —"

"I'll drive," Detective Fusilli says firmly.

As we get into his car, we draw closer to Zed. The police are doing that weird thing where they sort of help him into the car so that he won't bump his head. The gesture always seems tender to me, like what a mother would do.

I can see his face now. He doesn't look angry anymore. Just lost. He has a tattoo on his arm of a lily of the valley. The most delicate of flowers, little white bells.

The image of the tattoo and Zed's lost face fill me up with a gully wash of guilt that cuts a whole new stream of knowledge inside my brain.

His mother's name was Lily. I know that somehow. And I also know something else. The worry that fills him up isn't about Emily, it's about everything. It's about being a loser, it's about being lost. He is angry, withdrawn. But he didn't take Emily.

And there's another thing. The guy in my vision didn't have a tattoo.

I stop in my tracks as Joe Fusilli holds open the car door.

"He didn't do it," I say.

Joe Fusilli looks at me. I can tell I just got to the end of his last nerve. He sighs a sigh that seems to sum up every sleepless night he's had since this began. "Just get in the car," he says.

SIXTEEN

"She really tackled him?" Diego asks me the next morning.

We're in the kitchen. Diego is emptying the dishwasher. I am wiping down the counters. We occasionally intersect and do a neat dance, Diego's arms holding a plate over my head, my bumping closed a drawer for him with my hip. Disco chores.

"Like Boo Radley jumping the bad guy in *To Kill a Mockingbird*," I say.

"Hey, Boo," Diego says, and we giggle. Well. I giggle. Diego laughs.

"There's only one problem," I say. "Zed didn't do it."

Diego is stooping over the dishwasher. He straightens up. "What?"

"For one thing, he has a tattoo," I say. "In the vision, the guy carrying the dead girl doesn't have one."

"You said you didn't see him clearly."

"There were parts I saw clearly," I explain. "And I know there was no tattoo."

"So maybe the vision doesn't have to do with

Emily at all," Diego says. "You didn't recognize the girl."

"It may not be Emily, but I know it has to do with her," I say. "I just know it. It doesn't add up, Diego. Zed says that Emily had a crush on him, and he tolerated it. She was his boss's daughter. He loaned her a book. She's the one who made more out of it than there was."

"He says."

"I think she would have told me if there was something between her and Zed," I say. I stop wiping the counter, because I just might grind away the Formica. I turn and lean against it. "She might not have told me about a crush, but she would have told me about a thing."

"What about his computer?" Diego asks.

"He says he doesn't know how it got wiped," I explain. "And his dad says Zed doesn't know enough about computers to do it. Even *Rocky* has his doubts. He told Shay he can't believe it. Zed swore to him he doesn't know anything about Emily's disappearance."

"Are you forgetting that he tried to kidnap you?" Diego asks. He shuts the empty dishwasher.

"I don't know that." I've thought about what happened all last night. "He tackled me, and we fell down the hill. He wanted to know what the police had on him. He was *scared*. Angry, too, sure. Because I was the one who led them to him. I'd be plenty pissed, too, if I was innocent."

Diego doesn't try to argue with me. "So what should we do?"

"I don't know," I say. "I told Detective Fusilli all this, but he didn't care. The police think they have their guy. It's just a matter of getting more evidence."

"What does Shay think?"

"She saw him attacking me, or at least that's certainly the way it looked. The book is closed for her, too."

"Well, until we can figure out who did it, Zed is in trouble," Diego says.

"Well, Emily is in worse trouble. But finding her will help Zed."

"Exactly." He drums his fingers on the counter. "What about the oven? You saw that in your vision."

"Sort of."

"What about Rocky?"

"Emily's dad?"

Diego shrugs. "Nasty custody battle. It happens. Emily could be in another country by now, and Rocky is just cooling his heels, waiting to go."

"I hadn't thought of that."

"I bet the police have."

I shake my head. "This is all so confusing. I'm not a detective. But thanks."

"For . . ."

"Taking me seriously."

"No problem," Diego says. "Spook-doozy."

We hear Shay's footsteps. She walks into the kitchen, holding up a credit card. "Retail therapy," she says. "Anyone interested?"

"Mom," Diego says, "can I remind you of something? I'm a guy."

"Not tempting?"

"Not tempting."

"So what will you do today? It's Saturday."

"Guy things."

I watch them together. It's like I zoom backward, out of their space. There is something easy about the way they are together. Diego is seventeen. He has a relationship with Shay that I'll never have with my mother. I'll never have a relationship with Mom at seventeen, or nineteen, or twenty-three. We were just starting to have that thing where you're friends, when it's not just me looking up to her, but us looking at each other. I'll never get there. I'll never have the pleasure of watching us change. I'll be locked into Mom and me at fifteen.

Still grinning at Diego, Shay turns to me. "What do you say? Seattle? New clothes? I know all the cool stores in the U district."

What would Shay, Woman of Gauze, know about cool stores?

"Yes," Shay intones, noting my look of surprise, "I am a woman of fashion and mystery. Come."

The heat wave has broken, and the temperature is in the seventies when we hit the streets of Seattle. It's T-shirt weather, blue-sky weather, and everyone is out and grooving on it, because Satellites (which is what I call Seattle-ites) see most of the winter days through a frizzly, drizzly curtain of gray rain. Then mold starts growing on their sport mocs, and boom, it's summer.

I try to be enthusiastic about shopping, but I've got things on my mind. I can tell Shay does, too. We flip through racks of clothes but we can't get up the necessary self-interest to try anything on.

"This was a bad idea," Shay says finally.

I don't bother denying it. It feels weird to think about clothes when Emily is still missing.

"Let's go to Ballard and get Sno-Cones and look at the salmon ladder," Shay suggests. "That always makes me feel better."

"Okay," I agree, even though I have no idea what she's talking about. Motion seems like a good idea, though.

We're right near the University of Washington, the school everyone calls "U-Dub," which always sounds like the beginning of a nursery rhyme to me. We start walking down 45th Street, back toward the car. Students swirl around us, eating burritos as they walk, shouldering backpacks, talking about keg parties instead of chemistry. Shay suddenly stops outside a housewares store.

"Oh, I just remembered, I need a new cheese grater. Mine imploded the other day. Do you mind if we —"

"I'll wait outside." I'd much rather watch people than browse for cheese graters.

"It's a great store —"

"Shay? Not tempting."

She grins and goes inside.

I study the posters glued to the streetlamp. Concerts, yoga classes, a lecture on "The Porpoise-Driven Life: Lessons From Our Marine Friends," a night of "macrobiotic stand-up" at the Oat Harvest Health Restaurant.

And I think high school is wacky.

Behind the Oat Harvest flyer I see something. It's like I'm dreaming. It's a drawing. It's half of a white square, and flames are coming out of it.

Slowly, I tear off the Oat Harvest flyer. Underneath it, there is a logo. It is a computer monitor with flames licking out the top.

It is what I saw in my vision. I hadn't seen an oven. I had seen this.

COMPUTER CAMP FOR HIGH SCHOOL STUDENTS
SPONSORED BY MEGAWALL

I suddenly feel shaky. The day shifts, just like that, and the sidewalk seems to move under my feet. Suddenly, nothing seems as solid as it did a few seconds ago.

I read the flyer, faded from the weather and tattered from having other flyers tacked on top of it. It's the camp Emily got into, but couldn't attend.

I read the address, and it's only a few blocks away. And the camp is taking place now. I rip off the flyer and shove it in my pocket. Then I go into the store to find Shay.

She's got a grater tucked under her arm while she contemplates a roasting pan.

"Oh, Gracie, sorry, I get lost in these stores, I'll pay for this right —"

"No, it's okay," I say, trying to make my voice sound normal. "I found a store with some cool stuff. Can I meet you back here?"

"Ten minutes," Shay says.

"Fifteen?"

Her eye wanders and settles on something called a *bain-marie*. She holds it up. "Do I need this? I would feel very French if I had this."

"You could need it," I say. "That's what I'm thinking."

"Fifteen minutes," Shay says.

I walk out of the store.

I am thinking about the T-shirt I found in

Rocky's studio. I was holding the T-shirt when I got the vision of him. When I was inside his head. The T-shirt gave me the way in.

He had touched that shirt.

I start to run.

SEVENTEEN

I had promised Shay to tell her if I suspected anything, but that was before Zed was arrested. I know Shay wants to believe that the kidnapper has been caught, and she'll argue with me if I want to keep looking. After what happened in the parking lot, I know she'd tell me to let the police handle it.

But the police aren't handling it. They have Zed, and they're done. Besides, what kind of trouble could I get into at a computer camp full of kids?

What kind of trouble could you get into in a supermarket parking lot?

I tell myself to shut up and keep walking. The building is close to campus, one of those renovated warehouses with wood floors and big windows. I'm reassured at the sunlight pouring through the skylights as I step into the lobby.

The camp has taken over a suite of rooms on the second floor. I peek into the different rooms, which all empty out onto the hallway that winds around the building and overlooks the lobby. Kids are at computers while cool geeks stand over them or sit at their own computers. It's hard to tell the high school kids from the instructors, who look mostly college-age or a little older. There are tons of soda cans and balled-up bags of potato chips scattered on the long tables. There's a scoreboard for some kind of team game, divided into Team Rant and Team Rave. Pinned up on long bulletin boards are digitized photographs of President Bush with various vegetables on his shoulders instead of a head, and long sheets of code.

I'm not sure what I'm doing here, and I'm not sure what I'm looking for. All I know is that I have exactly twelve minutes to find it.

A tall boy with red hair stretches and cracks his knuckles like rifle shots, then pushes off from his computer. His wheeled chair shoots straight back into my knees.

"Ow!" I jump back and rub the area where two functional knees used to be.

He scrambles off the chair, almost falling in his eagerness. "Oh, man, I'm so fantastically sorry, are you okay?" He peers at me. His eyes are green behind his wire-rimmed glasses. Cute nerd. "File me under Idiot."

"No worries," I say. "Just a couple of knee replacements and I'll be fine."

"Can I help you, like, limp to a chair or something?"

"That's okay," I say. "I'm not staying. Just spying.

My friend got into this camp, but she wasn't able to come after all. I just wanted to check it out in case I want to apply next year."

"That would be awesome. I'm Ryan, by the way. Who's your friend?"

"I'm Gracie. My friend's name is Emily Carbonel."

"I thought so. When you said she couldn't come after all." Ryan looks eager. His breath smells like orange juice, and I see a carton of Tropicana on his desk. I step back a half-step. "How is Emily? I've e-mailed her a bunch of times, but I guess she got tired of my constant worship."

"She's missing," I say.

Ryan frowns. "Missing? Like, right now? You were supposed to meet her here?"

"No, I mean she's *missing*," I say. "The police think she was kidnapped."

"She didn't run away?" Ryan asks. "She was seriously bummed about her folks, I know that for sure."

"How do you know her so well?" I ask. "She wasn't able to come to the camp."

He nods. "Yeah, but I met her during the sign-up process, when a bunch of us came to check out the computers and stuff. And she came with her mom for orientation. That's when they found out that Emily's dad hadn't sent the check. Man, it was embarrassing. Emily was all teary, and it's lucky her mom couldn't get her hands on a ballistic missile. They left, and I found out on e-mail that her dad had spaced out and her mom didn't have the money to cover the cost, so they fought about it, and they missed the deadline, and somebody else got Em's slot. Major bummer for me."

"So you were friends with Emily?"

"Well, if you factor in my huge crush and her complete indifference to the basic fact of my existence," Ryan says. "She had a thing for somebody else."

I try not to pounce on this too obviously. "Do you know who?"

"No idea," Ryan says. "I didn't exactly press for romantic details."

A singsong voice comes from behind me. "I bet it's Mar-cus."

I turn around. A girl about my age is tilting a Diet Coke back to get the very last drop. She has cropped, sleek black hair and is wearing a tight T-shirt that says WHOA BABY. Her taut belly is already tan. It makes a long, slow slide into the low waistband of her jeans. I take an instant dislike to her belly button.

"Why do you think it's Marcus, Dora?" Ryan asks resentfully.

"Well, *ding-dong*. Obviously you haven't looked very hard."

"Who's Marcus?" I ask.

"She didn't even *know* Marcus," Ryan says. "She met him, like, maybe twice."

"Who's Marcus?"

"And how many times did you meet sweet Emily?" Dora cocks her head and widens her eyes at Ryan, and not in a nice way. She's making it clear that he's not in her league. I'm starting to like her less than her navel. "I've got a tip for you about your technique, Rye-bread. You're supposed to make the girl want to come to you, not run away. First Kendall, now Emma."

"Emily," I say.

Dora ignores me. I know she's needling Ryan because I'm there, but she's pretending I don't exist. Freeze the competition, humiliate the guy just for fun.

Ryan's cheeks are flushed. I feel sorry for him. He's no match for Dora. I have a feeling that neither am I.

"Emily and I talked online all the time," Ryan says defensively.

"So how do you know she didn't do that with Marcus, too?"

This stops Ryan for a moment, so I get in the question for the tenth time. "Who is Marcus?"

"He's one of the instructors," Ryan says glumly. "He's a sophomore at U-Dub. He's over there." He points with his chin.

I see a guy, maybe nineteen, sitting at a computer. He's got blond hair shaved down to stubble and a pair of black-framed glasses. He's wearing a white T-shirt that hugs his body *very* well. He looks like he has muscles on his cheekbones. I see what Dora means. He's good-looking, but he looks like Intenso Boy.

As if he's felt my gaze, he turns and sees me looking at him. He gives me a hard stare, then gets up and leaves the room.

"Ooooh, " Dora says. "See what I mean? Definitely hot."

Ryan gives the girl a sour look. "Not the kind of guy a girl like Emily would go for, Dora."

She crunches the can, and I notice that her navy-polished fingernails are bitten down, her cuticles red and angry-looking. "Right. Whatever you say. Anyway, what a waste of time. Why go for minnows when you have sharks? If you ask me, Jonah is the catch around here."

"Jonah? Jonah Castle?" Ryan breathes the name. "Are you delirious?"

Dora laughs.

"You haven't even met him. You didn't come on tour day."

"Who's . . ." I try.

Dora rolls her eyes. "I've seen his bank account."

"Who's Jonah Castle?" I ask.

"Who's Jonah Castle?" Ryan repeats, shocked.

I'm beginning to wonder if too much time in a digital mode makes for an inability to communicate with real people.

"Just your average unattached twenty-five-year-old dot-com billionaire," Dora-the-Ignorer says, finally acknowledging my existence. She walks off, tossing her can toward a trash can. Naturally, it goes in.

Ryan looks after Dora with, I'm sure, loathing in his heart. Who wouldn't?

He turns back to me. "Jonah Castle is a genius. He practically invented firewall software. At seventeen, he hacked into the top twenty of the Fortune 500, just to show them he could do it. They ended up buying firewall software from him. Megawall is his company."

"The sponsor of the camp."

"Right. Oh, that reminds me. Hang on." Ryan reaches for a backpack and rummages through it. He comes out with a photograph and shows it to me.

It's a photo of a group of kids, all wearing the red computer-camp T-shirt. They must have just gotten them, because I can see that most of them are wearing the shirt over their clothes. I spot Emily off to the left, next to Ryan. She has a big smile on her face, and she looks pretty. Marcus is there, on the other side of the group, looking aloof. He's standing next to a young-looking guy wearing a polo shirt and a tweed jacket. "That's Jonah Castle," Ryan says reverently, pointing to the man in the jacket. "This was taken on the tour day."

I take the photograph and stare at it. I feel my concentration slip from Ryan *into* the picture. I can feel Emily's happiness on that day, but I can feel other things, too, things that when I brush against them I'm afraid.

"Can I keep this?"

"I guess," he says reluctantly. "Just be sure and give it to Emily when she turns up. Hey, let me write my phone number on the back." Ryan takes the photograph and quickly scrawls on the back of it. He hands it back. "Listen, let me know if there's anything I can do, okay?" He fidgets, hands in his pockets, as if he's unused to offering help.

"Sure." I put the photograph carefully in my purse. I feel it there, weighing me down, as I walk out.

That photograph is like a rock in my purse for the rest of the afternoon. I can feel it with every step. We drive to the park by the locks and buy Sno-Cones from an Indian woman in a white truck. Then we cross over the locks and pause to look down, eating our Sno-Cones. We watch the water flood in as the boat slowly rises toward us, and Shay waves at the couple leaning against the stern rail.

Here is where the freshwater lake empties into the bay. We let the sea and the salt tangle in our lungs and our hair, and I know Shay feels her spirits lift, but she can't pull me along with her.

I stare down into the deck of the rising boat. It fills my vision, blocking everything out. Sound fades.

Hands are at the cabin window, beating against it.

First the palms slapping, then fists.

Trying to get out.

Have to get *out.*

No one will hear, no one saw

help me help me help me help me

"Gracie?"

The boat is level with us now. The curtains are parted, and I can see into the cabin. It is empty. A box of cookies sits on the dinette table. A sweatshirt is tossed on the seat.

"Gracie?" Shay's curls are blowing crazily. "You dropped your Sno-Cone."

I look down. The Sno-Cone has inverted and is sticking up like a pup tent.

The liquid oozes out on the concrete.

I reach out for the rail. It feels as though the ground is moving under my feet, and I'm dizzy.

Something is here, something I need to know, something I need to grasp.

It's gone.

It slips through my fingers, it sluices out through the locks. I lose it.

"Come on," Shay says. "Let's look at some fish."

We walk down the sloping lawn toward the salmon ladder. I see the flash of the fish even as we approach. We walk down the stairs and we're plunged into a gloomy dankness. We're surrounded by glass, and behind it, fish are swimming, slithering, battling the current. Some of them are cut and bloody. They throw themselves at a small opening, trying to get up into the sea. Again and again they make the leap, sometimes falling back, and always trying again.

I watch the salmon fight and flop their way upstream toward their eventual fate of being roasted or smoked or grilled on a cedar plank. I know I'm supposed to admire their determination, but they just seem so sad to me. Somewhere wired into their DNA is a memory of fresh water, smooth rocks, a still bay, and they'll fight their way past cities and chemicals and dams to find home. Instead they'll meet the hook and the net and be pulled, gasping, water streaming down their silvery gills, into the relentless air.

EIGHTEEN

The next morning in my room, I stare at the photograph for long periods of time, time enough to note that Emily's smile is a little too radiant, certainly more than a tour of computers would warrant, that Marcus is uncomfortable, that Jonah Castle has a cell phone in his left hand, like a busy executive making a dutiful visit to his charitable cause.

Something is wrong with this picture. I don't know what. Which gets me exactly nowhere.

Sunlight floods my room. Diego is in his bedroom, close by. There's nothing to be afraid of, and I'm afraid. There's a darkness in this photo. There's something there, just out of reach. I don't know what it is, but it has everything to do with Emily.

Lying with her eyes shut, afraid to move.

Someone standing in a doorway looking down at her, not caring who she is, only that she belongs with him.

Fists pounding against the cabin window of a boat.

help me help me help me

Who is the darkness coming from? Marcus?

He seems the obvious candidate, but maybe I'm making too many assumptions based on a shaved head and a bad attitude. Ryan? He admitted having a huge crush on Emily — are geeks capable of a criminal activity more serious than shoplifting a six-pack of Mountain Dew? Even Jonah Castle could be a suspect, I guess, though I can't quite imagine a billionaire taking time out from running a company to kidnap a teenager. It just doesn't make sense.

I fire up the online search engines. First I look up the website for the computer camp. There are several links, and they list each year's students, as well as the instructors. I see that Marcus Heffernan taught last year as well, and that he's a student at the University of Washington, just as Ryan said. Ryan attended the camp the year before, too. I scroll through the other names of the students, but nothing rings a bell. And then I see the name *Kendall Farmer.*

What about Kendall? You're supposed to make the girl want to come to you, not run away.

I click back on the search engine. I type in Kendall Farmer.

Article from the *Seattle Times,* October of last year.

Runaway Lead Turns Out False, Distraught Parents Report

I click on it and read the article, my eyes darting, wanting to pick up every piece of information.

I have to remind myself to slow down so I can absorb what I'm reading. Kendall Farmer disappeared last November, leaving a note for her parents that she was off to "find a family who cares." The police thought they had picked her up in San Diego, but it turned out to be a different kid.

Two missing girls, both of them connected to the computer camp. What were the odds of that?

I scroll through the rest of the results, reading everything. It's funny what oddball stuff comes up on a web search.

Kendall Farmer is mentioned in an article in the local paper of her hometown on Bainbridge Island. She'd played Marian in her school's production of *The Music Man,* and the reviewer praises her "lovely singing voice and stage presence."

Her parents gave a pot luck on August 17th of last year to benefit the library. Kendall presented the proceeds of the annual Car Wash Jive from her high school.

She won second prize on Get Up and Prove It Night at the Smells Like Good Coffee Café in Seattle.

She sounds like a normal kid. She is still missing. She is sixteen.

I look back at the photograph. In Marcus's neutral face, I think I read obsession. Is the darkness I feel coming from him?

I have to find out.

I cross through the kitchen and then mosey down the hall. Diego's door is open, and I hover in the doorway until he notices me. He's listening to music on his headphones and chatting online.

He lifts one earphone when he sees me.

"Want to go on a stakeout?" I ask.

Marcus Heffernan turns out to be a rich kid. He lives in a million-dollarish house that backs onto Lake Washington. We park the car outside and wait. The only problem is, I have no idea what we're waiting for. But we do it for an hour. We finish a bag of donuts ("for atmosphere," Diego says) and put the CD player on random.

"This is fun," Diego says. His voice doesn't exactly ring with sincerity.

Okay, so stakeouts are boring. Who knew? They go by so fast on TV.

I feel responsible for Diego's boredom, but I have no idea how to entertain him. I had to talk him into coming. First of all, he's not allowed to drive to Seattle without permission, but I point out that Shay is in meetings all day and can't talk to us anyway. It's pretty lame, but it eases his conscience a little bit. Then it turns out that he doesn't *want* to drive to Seattle. He has an intermediate license, which means if he gets even two tickets, his license is suspended. I don't think Diego is afraid of anything, but if he is, it's of not having a car.

He drums his fingers on the dash. He shifts in his seat. He clears his throat.

"So . . ." he says.

"So . . ."

"So why did you hire that guy to punch you?"

I look out the window. It's funny. My life here seemed so unreal to me for so long. But Diego's question takes me by surprise, because suddenly *that* life seems far away, my life in Maryland after Mom died, when every day I woke up and had to talk myself into swinging my legs over the side of the bed.

"Because I wanted to feel pain that wasn't inside me," I say. "I thought if I could focus on a different kind of pain, even for a few minutes, I could feel . . . I don't know, relief. I could be the me I was before, even temporarily."

"Did it work?" He asks the question so delicately, as though he were a doctor probing a wound, which I guess he is.

"No," I say. "I just felt pretty stupid, basically. And Jake Buscemi just felt really bad. I think he was surprised that he actually did it. Me, too."

"You freaked everyone out," Diego says.

"Yeah." Myself included, actually. That was one bad day.

"They wanted to maybe put you somewhere for a while," Diego says.

This gets my attention. "What? Like a mental institution?"

Diego nods. "Mom talked them out of it. She put her foot down. Threatened to call in lawyers and everything. They had talked her out of taking you right after . . . right after, and she gave in because she thought they might be right. That it wasn't a good idea to remove you from everything you knew."

I thought Shay hadn't wanted me. I thought she'd refused. Maybe they'd told me the way it really was. I couldn't remember. I wasn't listening to anyone then.

"So anyway, you know Pop-Pop and Mimi, they always get their way. And Uncle Owen always sides with them, so Mom was outgunned. But after that thing happened, and they were all wondering what to do, Mom called and told them she wouldn't take no for an answer, that your mom had wanted you to come live with us, and that's how it had to be. We'd already redone the room, that summer."

"You did my room last summer?"

"Yeah. In case you ever wanted to come. Anyway, they caved."

"I thought I was too much for Mimi and Pop-Pop."

"Well, you were." Diego chuckled. "That's for sure. They freak when they get rained out of the ninth hole, so you can imagine."

It was true. My grandparents are seriously stuck in their ways. If they run out of seven-grain bread at the supermarket, my grandfather wants to file a lawsuit. And everything has to be just so. Spoons go handle *down* in the dishwasher, forks go handle *up*. Shoes *off* when you come in the door. Wipe the cast-iron frying pan with paper towel *only*. Up, down, top, bottom, off, on, only, never, always. I never understood their rules, and they tried to be nice, but they were always redoing everything I did. Maybe it added to my craziness then, I don't know. But I never felt right. It was the first time in my life I realized that love wasn't enough to help somebody.

"They are serious about toilet paper," I say. "At first, I didn't notice. It took me weeks to get it. If I put it on the roll with the paper coming from the bottom of the roll, they'd flip it over. Toilet paper has to come from the *top* of the roll."

"When I visited them, I used to keep switching it back, just to drive them nuts," Diego says.

We burst out laughing.

With Diego poking fun at them in that genial way, I realize for the first time that flunking out of the grandparent living situation wasn't totally my fault. They *are* kind of nuts. It wasn't my fault that I couldn't fit into their particular brand of craziness. Each family is weird in its own way, I guess, which makes it hard to find your way in a new one.

"There's our boy," Diego says. He starts the engine.

Marcus walks out of the house, jingling car keys. He's wearing a gray T-shirt with lettering I can't read and khaki shorts and boots. If I weren't a detective, I would notice his legs in a much less clinical way. He hops into a Volkswagen Beetle and backs out of the driveway.

I duck my head down until Diego says it's okay. Then we proceed to tail Marcus through the unfamiliar streets of Seattle, through stop signs and red lights. I learn that Diego knows how to curse.

Marcus stops at a gas station (I duck; Diego curses and keeps going, turns right; it's a one-way street; we have to circle and get back, hoping Marcus needs a full tank of gas; we spot him as he zooms through a yellow light . . .), gets caught in a traffic jam (we keep four cars back), and then cruises in the U district, looking for a parking space. He finds one and pulls in.

"What now?" I ask. I look around, but there are no spaces. Marcus is already getting out of the driver's seat.

"Follow him," Diego says.

"But how will you find me?"

"Send me a text message. If I don't find you or hear from you in fifteen minutes, I'm calling Detective Pasta. Now *go*."

I scoot out the door and bound onto the sidewalk. I keep well behind Marcus. It's easy to keep him in sight. He's tall and he's not walking very fast, chugging on a bottle of sports drink as he goes.

He disappears into the doorway of a restaurant. My palms are wet. I wipe them on my jeans, then walk slowly up to the window. I give a quick look in.

Marcus has his back to me. He stops and reads a blackboard with the specials on it. Then he walks behind the counter and picks up an apron, which he ties around his waist. I don't know how he manages it, but he looks pretty macho in it.

He's a waiter. I watch him for a few minutes. He says something to the waitress that makes her smile. He disappears into the kitchen and comes back out. I study his face. I wait for something to break inside me, some kind of flash that will tell me what I need to know.

When Diego's hand hits my shoulder, I jump about six inches.

"Whoa. What's going on?"

"He went to work," I say. "I guess we can go home. He'll be here for a while." I feel discouraged. This isn't getting me anywhere. I have a sense of urgency now, that Emily is in trouble, that she needs me. I've got to find a way to link Marcus to Emily, or I have to find another suspect.

"Come on," Diego says. "We'll think of something else. This smells like teen washout." He points overhead.

"What?" I look up at the sign hanging overhead.

The name of the café is Smells Like Good Coffee. I had been concentrating so hard on Marcus, I hadn't noticed it.

The Smells Like Good Coffee Café. Where Kendall Farmer won second prize on Get Up and Prove It Night.

"It's him," I say, latching onto Diego's arm. "He's our guy."

NINETEEN

"Let's not jump to conclusions," Diego says, after I explain the connection. "Emily and Kendall both knew Marcus. So what?"

"The coincidences are piling up," I argue. "What are the odds of two girls disappearing when they know the same guy? And the person who wiped those computers was an expert. It went way beyond sending stuff to the recycle bin."

Diego sighs. "We have to be careful, Gracie. You were certain about Zed."

He's right. But that doesn't mean I like hearing it. Time is running out for Emily. I can feel it now, and I realize it's been there the whole day. While we were driving to Seattle, while we were talking in the car, I was feeling it.

She's giving up.

She's slipping away.

And the answers are in front of me. I've seen the clues.

I've been inside his head.

"She's given up trying to be brave," I say. "She's given up waiting to be rescued. She's . . . fading."

"What?" Diego asks.

"Emily. I feel her emptying out. So that" — my mouth is dry — "so that when the worst happens, she won't feel it."

Diego looks shaken. "Maybe if you had something of Marcus's, something he owned . . ."

"Maybe I'd get a vision!" I say. "It's worth a shot."

We're only blocks from the computer camp, and I know they don't start until noon. Diego and I hurry toward it. We push through the doors and run up the stairs to the second floor. All the classrooms are locked.

"What now?" I ask, frustrated. "Should we try to break in?"

Diego sighs. He raises his hand and knocks.

"Or I guess we could try knocking," I say.

The door opens. Ryan's head appears. He brightens when he sees me, then frowns when he sees Diego standing next to me.

"This is my cousin Diego," I say.

Ryan brightens again. "I came in early to get some work done. Come on in."

"How come you have a key?" I ask.

"The instructors give us one if we ask," Ryan explains. "You have to sign in and stuff. Hey, what brings you here?"

I hadn't had much time to prepare a story, so I thought a mixture of truth and fiction was best. "I'm really worried about Emily," I tell him. Truth.

"I guess I was kind of distracted yesterday. I think I left my sunglasses here." Fiction. "Can I look around?"

"Sure. Can I help?"

Diego smiles at Ryan. "That's okay. We don't want to interrupt." He says this firmly, and disappointed, Ryan sits back down at his computer.

I pretend to look around, and Diego stays between me and Ryan so Ryan won't have a good sight line. I drift toward the desk where Marcus had been working, but it's clear of anything, even empty soda cans. Then I see a row of mailboxes with names on them — the names of the instructors. Marcus's is full to overflowing.

Bending down and pretending to look on the floor, I rifle through the pages. Memos, mostly, and takeout menus, and assignments handed in by the students. Then I see a corner of a photograph. I slide it out. It's the same photograph Ryan had given me.

Something clangs in my head. Something's wrong. Somewhere behind me, I can hear Diego sneezing, and I wish he'd stop, because I can't concentrate.

Suddenly, Ryan reaches down and takes the photograph.

"It was on the floor," I say.

His face is red, as though he's angry. "Jonah Castle gave us each a copy," he says. "This must belong to Marcus." He quickly stuffs it back in the mailbox.

Diego knocks over a pile of circuits, and Ryan yells, "Hey!" and runs over. Quickly, I stuff the photograph in my purse. I dig out my sunglasses.

"Found them! I must have kicked them under the desk. Thanks so much, Ryan." I pour as much flirtatiousness as I can manage into my thank-you, but Ryan doesn't respond. His head is down as he reassembles the circuits, and he mumbles a good-bye.

As soon as we're outside, I turn to Diego. "You could have warned me Ryan was coming."

"I did! I sneezed!"

"What kind of a signal is a sneeze?"

"A *clever* one."

"A sneeze isn't a signal; it's an allergic reaction."

"Great. Next time I'll fart."

Suddenly, I realize what it must be like to grow up with an older brother. I take out the photograph.

There's something different about it. What?

And then I get it.

"Emily's not here," I say. I shake my head, confused. "She's gone."

Diego looks over my shoulder. "Where was she?"

"Here, next to Ryan. Now there's just empty space."

"So they took two photographs that day," Diego says.

"But everyone has the same expression. And Jonah Castle is still holding the cell phone in the same position. No, this is the same one." I look up at Diego. "Someone digitally altered it. They *removed* her." I shivered.

"The question is, who?" Diego says.

"It was in Marcus's box."

"But Ryan looked really freaked."

"He always looks freaked."

We walk to the car and get in. Diego starts the engine. I stare back down at the photograph. The absence of Emily registers as a presence. It's like the ghost of her is there, the ghost of the Emily that is fading, and it's saying, *find me.*

TWENTY

Shay makes spinach lasagna that night. I eat two helpings and then drag myself to my room, ready to fire up Google once again.

Shay appears in my doorway. "Want to catch some mindless TV for the masses?"

"No thanks," I say. "I'd rather use the computer."

"Okay." Shay smiles, but I can tell she's disappointed. I almost feel like changing my mind and losing myself in a laugh track, but my brain is burning to hit the Internet for info, and I just can't take a detour. The feeling I got today about Emily pushes out everything except this need to find her.

I've turned Shay down for so many things over the past months. TV, movies, Scrabble, hikes, pedicures at the day spa. I don't know why tonight I feel badly about saying no. I guess it's because she keeps trying.

I log online and plug Marcus into the search engine. I don't exactly hit paydirt. I get the website of the computer camp, but I knew that already. And apparently, Marcus writes for the campus newspaper, because a bunch of articles pop up, but none of them look as though they have even a remote connection to Emily or Kendall, dull stuff about school policy, off-campus lectures, and a couple of film reviews.

Then, back in July of last year, I see something interesting.

Interview with Jonah Castle.

At least I might learn more about the computer camp. I click on the link.

I quickly scan the article. It's all about how Jonah Castle funded the computer camp to help gifted students. Out of all his charities, this is the one close to his heart. He was a prodigy and he knows how lonely it can be. Blah, blah, blah. It all sounds so canned. Potential. Encouragement. Leadership. Synergy. Dreams. Values. The usual.

Q: You had an unusual childhood. You were home-schooled, you had eleven brothers and sisters, and your family lived on a private island in Puget Sound. Has your upbringing influenced the way you look at education today?

A: It's funny. I don't see my childhood as unusual. Does anyone? It's your reality, and you don't have anything to compare it to. I consider myself lucky to have been homeschooled by my parents, who were brilliant scholars and imaginative teachers. Each of my siblings was encour-

aged to develop a specific skill. My sister Frances was an accomplished vocalist. My brother Tate was an outstanding mathematician. Another sister played the clarinet. Our playtime always involved our studies, and our family fun always had an educational element.

Q: In other words, you weren't hanging out watching South Park.

A: No, we were reading aloud, or putting on our own entertainments. We were off the grid, anyway.

Q: Sounds like a pretty cool childhood.

A: It was.

Sorry, Jonah Castle, but your childhood sounds like a snooze fest.

Diego pops his head in the doorway. "Eureka, I found it."

"Found what?"

"The original photograph. Megawall has its company newsletter archived online. I printed it out. Here."

He hands me the photograph. It's identical to the one I took from Marcus's mailbox. No Emily.

"So what does it mean?" I wonder. "Did someone scan Emily *in* or scan her *out?*"

"I've got one way to find out." Diego hands me the phone. "Call Ryan."

"But if he's involved, he'll lie."

"We've got to take that chance. At least, we'll be doing *something.*"

I read Ryan's number off the back of the photo he gave me and punch it out. He answers on the first ring. When I explain who I am, he says, "Wow, I never thought you'd call. I mean, I hoped you'd call. But I never —"

"Ryan, I saw the photograph today in Marcus's box."

"Yeah," he says cautiously.

"Emily isn't in it, but she's in the one you gave me."

"Yeah."

I wait.

"Okay. We got a pile of photos from Megawall? And they had edited out Emily because she wasn't in the camp after all? The photo goes out for publicity and everything, so I guess they wanted it to be accurate. So that made me feel bad, and I thought that it would be a nice present if I gave her a photograph with her in it. I'd taken a photo of her that day wearing the shirt. So I scanned the photo and scanned her in. It was just to make her happy, okay?"

"Oh. Okay. I was just wondering. So, she was in the original picture?"

"Yeah, she was standing on the right, next to Marcus. I just moved her over next to me. You know, I don't want you to think that I'm still in heavy crush over Emily. I'm, you know, available."

"That's great, Ryan." I make a sign to Diego that we're back at square one. Emily's disappearance from the photo has nothing to do with the fact that she's missing. It was just a publicity decision.

"What I mean is, we could have coffee or something."

"Great. I'll call you." I hang up. I toss the photo on my desk and tell Diego about the conversation.

"I guess it's slightly demented, but normal," Diego says. "He's a geek with a crush. That's why he flamed out when you found it — he was embarrassed, that's all. We just need to keep digging. Something will turn up." Diego ducks out again.

I reach over for the photograph again. I stare hard at Marcus. Emily had been standing next to him in the original. Now she was gone. Could Marcus have had something to do with it, despite what Ryan said? I wish I could get a feeling that was true. All I feel is confusion.

I try to walk my brain outside what I know. I try to tune into what I feel, or rather, what's *beyond* what I feel. I have to get control of the visions. I'm tired of them sneaking up on me and giving me a wallop. I have to make it happen, not wait for it to happen.

I stop staring at the photograph. I just look at it. I push every fear, every thought out of my mind and replace it with . . . nothing. Not even static.

The photograph doesn't make sense anymore as people and desks, just as shapes and colors.

The photograph dissolves into dots. The dots jiggle and swim. It's a jarring thing, and nothing comes into focus for a moment.

Then I'm walking on a beach. I'm surrounded by mist. I am carrying something. It is heavy.

It is a body.

I am chilled to the bone. I look down at the face of the girl.

She is sleeping. Please let her be sleeping.

Then the girl sits up and smiles. Blood drips from her mouth.

I scream and drop her on the shells. The sharp edges cut her skin. She bleeds and smiles.

And then the scene shifts, and the shells turn into grass, and I see small children running. They are bending to look at things: flowers and bugs. There is a garden, and a bench. It's like I'm watching from a distance this time. A girl is sitting on the bench. Not Emily, but someone I know. I can't see her face, but she is familiar to me. She is waiting for someone. I see the shadows of the trees fall on the grass. There is something white on the bench next to her — it looks like a party hat.

He is watching her, too. He is waiting.

Footsteps approach her.

Run, I tell her. *Run.*

I know something terrible will happen. I am watching now, but I can't move. She sees someone coming.

Run. Get out of there!

But she doesn't move, and then suddenly I see water churning, close-up, and I smell gasoline, heavy and sweet. I feel sick, and my face is wet and my hands are wet. I touch my tongue to my lip and taste blood . . .

"Gracie."

The word penetrates the mist. I grab onto the word as if it is a grasping hand and can pull me up. "Gracie!"

I am looking up at Diego's face. He is directly over me. His eyes are so black, so dark. I am afraid I will fall into them the way I fell into the mist. I'm afraid I will never come back from his gaze.

He grips my arms. "You scared me. What happened? What did you see?"

I realize I am lying back on my bed. My face is wet with perspiration. My neck is wet. I touch my lip and then look at my fingers, but there is no blood, of course. I shakily try to sit. Diego helps me.

"What did you see?" he asks urgently again. There is fear on his face.

I tell him what I saw, trying to remember every detail.

"You couldn't see the guy's face, or anything? Think. His shoes? His hands?"

"Nothing. Just his shadow." I cover my face with my hands. "When I saw the girl, the dead one, on the beach, I was seeing through his eyes. It was horrible. I think he killed her, Diego!"

He bites his lip. "Was it . . ."

"It wasn't Emily. It could have been Kendall. I don't know!"

"Was it the future, or the past?"

"I don't know."

"What about when you smelled gas, and you touched your lip . . . who were you then? Emily?"

"I don't know," I say, shaking my head. "I don't know!" I tell him about the other vision, about the fists beating against the window of the boat.

"Was that Emily? Remember, you saw her on the boat."

I'm tired of saying "I don't know." So I just look at him helplessly.

"It's okay. It's okay." Diego pats my shoulder lamely. "It's just in your head."

"Isn't that where all the bad stuff is?" I whisper. "Just in our heads?"

Diego clears his throat. "Let's analyze what you saw. What about the party hat? What could that mean?"

"Who knows? I just know that she's his next victim, whoever she is. He's going to take another girl. I saw her." Diego is trying to be logical, but I'm frantic. Panic thrums inside me like vibrating strings. I clutch his arm. "We have to stop him. It's up to us."

"We'll go to the police . . ."

"With what? A vision? A photograph?" I shake my head. "We have to get to the girl before he does."

Diego shakes his head. "Gracie, I don't know. This has gone far enough. We should . . . tell someone again. Shay . . ."

"They won't listen to me! And I know it's going to happen again."

"But you don't know where or when."

But even as he says this, the knowledge roars into my brain. "Yes I do. It wasn't a party hat," I say. "It was a Sno-Cone."

"A Sno-Cone?"

I am already reaching for the computer, typing fast. I run the search engine and find the site I'm looking for.

"Gracie —"

The official website of Seattle Parks and Recreation. I quickly click and scroll. Then I push the computer toward him so he can read what's on the screen.

Toddler Nature Hunt. 11 A.M. Saturday. Commodore Park.

"The park by the fish ladder," I tell Diego. "That's the place. They sell Sno-Cones there. It's going to happen this Saturday. That's where he'll be. I know it, Diego. I know it."

This time I am certain. And I know I have to be there, too.

TWENTY-ONE

I don't know how I talk Diego into it, but I do. There's no danger, I tell him. It's a public park! There will be two- and three-year-olds running around with their parents! It will be broad daylight! And most of all, I tell him, hammering the point home until he begs for mercy, we *know* what we're heading into. Whoever that girl is that I saw on the bench — she doesn't have a clue.

Technically, Shay hasn't given Diego permission to take the car to Seattle. Okay, *definitely*, Shay hasn't given permission. Diego isn't crazy about not telling her again. He got away with it once, but he doesn't want to push it. That's the toughest part of convincing him. He just doesn't lie to his mom. Ever. I'm not sure why he gives in, but he does.

We don't say much on the drive. Even though there's nothing to be nervous about in a certain way, there's everything to be nervous about in another way, so we just sit, listening to the radio and vibrating along with the tunes and our nerves.

We park. We hang out by the Sno-Cones for a while, seeing if a young girl buys one, but only a couple of people come by.

"Let's scout out the bench," Diego says.

We walk through the gardens, looking at the benches. When I see the one that was in my vision, I stop dead. There's something so real about it. I've never been in this part of the park with Shay, but I know this bench. I know the texture of the wood and the curve of the slats. This is the first time that something in my vision really comes true, something I can see. The pattern of the leaves overhead, the trampling of the grass in front, everything is just as I had seen it. It spooks me.

"This one?" Diego asks. He looks kind of spooked, too.

I nod.

Toddlers are beginning to arrive in the gardens, along with their parents. A pair of guides appear and start talking about "nature's marvelous wonders." They speak in that overly animated way that people do when they're around kids, and most of the toddlers are ignoring them while their parents are enthralled. The parents keep trying to drum up their kid's enthusiasm, saying, "Listen to the nice man, Dylan!" and "Remember how much you like ladybugs, Marina!" The sun is filtering through the leaves, and suddenly it seems like the worst thing that could possibly happen here would be a two-year-old throwing a tantrum.

The toddler pack moves off down the path, but

we can hear them. We stand there for a moment, but it's obvious that we can't remain.

We can't scare off whoever is coming.

"We'd better keep moving," Diego says. "If we stay between here and the entrance to the garden, nobody can get around us. If only we had a toddler for protective coloration."

I bend down and pick up one of the brochures that a parent had dropped. I hand it to Diego. "Try this. At least you don't have to buy it ice cream."

There's a place to hang by the entrance where we can stay behind some trees. I fidget. The shadows on the ground are telling me that this is it, this is the time my vision took place.

I see someone familiar heading toward us.

To my surprise, it's Dora.

I elbow Diego and point.

"She's in the computer camp," I say.

I notice now that she's eating a Sno-Cone. I feel a shiver rise all along my body.

We're on the right track after all.

Dora doesn't notice me. She walks past us, looking at her watch.

She is meeting someone.

Diego and I give each other a "what should we do now" look.

"I'll go scope out Dora," I say. "You stay here. If you see Marcus or Ryan, follow him."

Diego frowns. "Be careful. Is your cell phone on?"

"It's on." We've already decided to call each other only in an emergency. I take off down the path.

Dora sits on the bench, eating her Sno-Cone. I stop. She hasn't seen me yet, and I could keep going and pass her by, but I can't.

I tell myself Dora can take care of herself.

I tell myself that the important thing is to wait to see who shows up.

But I see her bitten fingernails around the white cone, how her toes are dirty in her sandals, and suddenly I can *feel* her as well as I see her.

I know her unhappiness is deep and wide.

I know that her mother is an alcoholic.

I see Dora, wearing a short nightgown, pick her mother off the floor and put her to bed.

I know that she thinks she's at a dead end, and this is her only way out.

She spots me. I could have waved and walked away, but I come forward.

"Hi."

"Hey."

Not a promising start. I sit on the bench. "Nice day."

She half-turns. "Look, hello and everything, but I'm meeting someone, so if you don't mind?"

"Who are you meeting?"

"Excuse me, are you my mother?" Dora asks nastily.

"Just making conversation."

"Don't bother. Do you *mind*?"

Dora leans over and dumps out the rest of her Sno-Cone. I am not surprised when she doesn't crumple it up. She puts the empty cone down on the bench upside down, like a tent, just the way it was in my vision. She slams it down as though she's marking her territory, making a kind of barrier between us.

I look down at the cherry ice seeping into the ground. The red color is so intense. The stain grows in my mind and I flash into the vision of the blood on the beach.

And suddenly, I know this:

Dora has to get out of here.

"You've got to go," I say.

Dora narrows her eyes. She has lined them with black pencil, and she's wearing lipstick. She has fixed herself up.

"Is it Marcus? Is it Ryan? Who is it?"

"What is *wrong* with you?" she asks, leaning back to put distance between us.

"Tell me who it is!"

"It's Marcus," she says. "Jealous?"

Marcus. It is Marcus.

"Listen, I'm psychic," I say. "Really. And I see things."

She smirks. "You see dead people?"

"I see your mother lying on the kitchen floor," I say. "She needs help, and you can't give it. You can't save her. You tried and now you're just angry."

Her expression changes. "Hey . . ."

"Your kitchen has an orange sink," I say. "Your nightgown has yellow flowers. You have a birthmark on your knee. A butterfly tattoo in the small of your back. Once your mother left you alone for two weeks, and you didn't tell anyone because you were afraid she was dead."

"Nobody knows that," Dora says, a look of fear on her face. *"Nobody knows that."*

"Your dishtowels have green stripes," I say. "Your dish drainer is white. Your mother's blanket is blue."

She is pressed back against the bench now. "What do you want?"

"Get out of here," I say. "Run. What do you think happened to Kendall and Emily? If you see him, don't stop." The danger is like the roar of surf in my ears. *"Get out of here!"*

Dora shoots to her feet. She gives me a last look, and then she takes off. Running. I don't know if she's spooked by me, or my warning. It doesn't matter.

I notice that my hands are trembling. I tuck them in my armpits. I expect Diego to show up at any moment, running, to tell me that Marcus has entered the park.

But instead, Jonah Castle rounds the bend, sees me, and smiles.

"Dora?" he says.

TWENTY-TWO

"I thought Marcus was coming," I say.

"He's at the party," he says.

"Oh," I say. What party?

He settles down on the bench next to me, giving the empty cone a brief, puzzled glance. "It's good to meet you. Marcus says you might need help."

My brain is buzzing like a hive. I've got to keep following this, but I'm lost. I try to come up with Dora's defensive attitude. "Not really."

He smiles pleasantly. He's got a narrow face, and his eyes are bright blue and interested behind his wire rims. He's wearing a polo shirt and pleated khakis, standard nerd attire. Boat shoes and white socks. I try to get something from him, some kind of wave, the way I've done with strangers. Sometimes people have something that is so present on their minds that I can just pick it up like a radio station. But Jonah Castle is a blank. I can't get anything from him.

"Oh, okay," he says genially. "I guess he got it wrong. Marcus is a mysterious guy."

"I'll say."

"He said you were upset at camp the other day," he says. "He wants to help, that's all."

"The way he helped Kendall Farmer?"

He looks blank. "Kendall Farmer? Should I know her?"

"She was in the camp last year," I say. "She ran away."

"Oh. And Marcus tried to help her? I'm not surprised, he's such a good guy."

You think so?

"I'm sorry, I didn't know. Marcus never mentioned her to me." He hooks two hands around a knee. "I lost a sister, you know. So I know about loss. Guilt. All that stuff. I know how bad feelings can grow inside you until they feel like they can eat you alive. I know how scary that can be, and how the fear can add to it until you just want to run and run to get away. But there's no place to run to. You know that saying, 'Wherever you go, there you are'?"

No, I don't know it. But I like how true it is. I'm listening now.

"So I started this thing, this focus group foundation. I mean, Megawall has the computer camp, and other charities, but my foundation doesn't get any publicity. I don't want reporters around, poking into people's privacy. I'm out to revolutionize how social services treat at-risk kids. I've got scholars and shrinks on the payroll, but mostly it's the kids themselves who have come up with the ideas.

Bright kids like you. When I asked Marcus if he knew anyone I could talk to, he mentioned you. I hope you don't mind."

"My life is none of his business," I say.

"No, it isn't. And if you don't want to get involved, I'd appreciate it if you didn't get mad at Marcus. Remember, I'm his boss, in a way." Jonah Castle smiles. "I can't deny that even if I don't use my leverage, it's there."

I can't get a read on this guy. Never mind the paranormal, the normal me can't read him, either. I feel apprehensive, but I don't know if I can connect the feeling to Jonah Castle. Everything about him tells me that he's an ordinary mega-billionaire looking to unload some millions on charity so he can sleep at night. But somehow he's connected to Marcus, and Marcus asked Dora to meet him here.

Could Jonah Castle's foundation be the key? Marcus directs troubled kids to the foundation. But not all of them. Some of them, he keeps for himself. Maybe he'd targeted Dora, only Jonah Castle got in his way.

It's hard to think and carry on a conversation at the same time. I focus back on Jonah Castle. "I don't think of myself as an at-risk kid," I say. "At risk for what?"

He laughs. "Yeah, here I am saying social services is messed up, and I'm using their terms. Let's just say this: You need a home where you can feel safe."

That breaks like a wave of longing inside me. Those two words. *Home. Safe.* When those two things get taken away from you, there's no other feeling more desolate. Maybe Jonah Castle knows what he's talking about.

"Listen," he says. "We're having a party for the third anniversary of the foundation. Most of the kids we've helped will be there. It's right in the park — that's why Marcus suggested this place to meet. Would you like to come?"

My antenna is up, but it's not picking up danger. There will be plenty of people there. Jonah Castle will be there, other adults. Diego is nearby.

My cover will be blown if Marcus sees me, but I don't care. I'll make something up. I'll say I pretended to be Dora so I could go to the party.

"I just need to call my cousin and tell him," I say.

"Sure. Ask him if he wants to come."

I flip open my cell, but I get NO SERVICE on the screen. We hadn't checked our phones when we arrived. Stupid.

He peers over. "Happens all the time. If we walk a bit, you can try again."

"Okay." I get up. Diego is probably watching us right now. And I can call again. I can hear the children running through the grass, and I can see the parents now, chasing after them. I'm fine, I'm safe, Diego would tell me to keep going.

"Great." He stands up and starts down the path.

We'll pass right by Diego, but that's good. Diego can tail us.

We get to the entrance of the gardens, and Jonah looks around. I do, too, but I don't see Diego. I figure he's lurking behind a lilac bush, watching.

"Shoot," Jonah says, and looks at his watch. "It's later than I thought. They must be on the boat already."

"Boat?" Everything lights up now. I'm close. I'm so close.

"Marcus has a boat. Well, his parents do."

Marcus has a boat. *That's it,* I think. *That's how he gets them away.* Marcus invited her out on the boat. At first, she's happy, he's going fast, and the wind is whipping her hair. But something happens, somehow he gets her down in the cabin, and she panics.

I have to see the boat. I have to get on board. If I can just touch it, see it, be in that space, I can pick up something. I know it.

"Do you know the marina? It's a short walk from here."

"Let's go." I don't have a real feeling about what is going to happen, but I do have a real feeling. It is that somehow Emily is calling me. She's telling me, *follow.*

So I follow. It's almost as though I don't care what's at the end.

I just have to find it.

TWENTY-THREE

We cross the locks, and then the parking lot. We start up Seaview Avenue. Jonah Castle tells me about the park, how it started, how a group of neighborhood people got together and made it happen. That's what he believes in, he says. A group of people with a common bond get together and things happen. It's how he built his company, he says. Just a bunch of friends fooling around in a garage with some software. Just to see what would happen.

I guess it's kind of cool, talking to a major cyber-pioneer, a legend. I'm thinking that the Maryland friends I'm not so in touch with anymore deserve an e-mail about this.

We get to the marina. The sunlight scampers on the water. We walk down toward the docks. There are people here, sitting on their boats. They wave at us and smile.

We walk down a dock all the way to the end. He stops in front of a big cabin cruiser, about forty feet long. "I think this is it. Let me check it out." He jumps aboard while I wait on the dock. I look behind me, but I don't see Diego.

He disappears inside the cabin. Then he pokes his head out. "Marcus isn't here. But . . ."

"What?" I ask. Jonah looks worried.

"It looks like the boat has been broken into or something," he says. "There's stuff all over the floor, and —"

He stops.

"What?"

"You'd just better stay there. I'll call Marcus. No, I'll call 911." He takes out his cell phone, then slaps the side of the canvas flap in frustration. "No service. Let's walk back to . . ."

I'm not waiting for the police. I have to get aboard. I have to feel the space, touch it. The police can find clues. But they can't find what I can *feel*.

I spring onto the boat.

"Don't," he warns, taking a step toward me. "They won't want anyone else aboard."

But I evade him. I have to look. He doesn't want to tell me what he saw, but I have to see it. I know that a thief didn't break in. I know that Jonah has seen signs of a struggle. Something happened on this boat.

I had seen the fists pounding.

I had felt her panic like it was my own.

It's as if I'm in a dream, a dream that someone else has dreamed. I can see the white deck, the bright snapping blue flag. And Emily is saying, *keep going. Help me, help me.*

I bend forward to look into the cabin. The surprise that it is neat, nothing out of place, is still registering dully in my head when I feel his hands on my back, when the push sends me down the stairs.

I land on my hands and knees, but I bite my lip hard.

I hear the *thunk* of the door.

My face is in the carpet. I am stunned. My lip is bleeding. I touch my tongue to the blood.

No.

Under my cheek, I feel the engines start up.

No.

I run to the window. I can't open it.

I smell gasoline and see churning foam.

I pound on the window with my palms, slap them against the window. Then I use my fists.

"Help me, help me, help me!" I scream the words, over and over.

No one can hear.

My vision swims into focus. The girl on the bench, waiting.

I had been right all along about the danger.

Now I see it clearly.

The girl I had seen on the bench wasn't Dora at all.

The girl I had seen on the bench was me.

TWENTY-FOUR

When we are far out on the Puget Sound, he comes downstairs. By now I am sitting at the table in the dining area. My lip is swollen, and I haven't wiped off the blood. Somehow I want him to see it. I want him to see what he's done.

I've tried my cell phone a hundred times. No Service.

I am so afraid that my body is rigid. I am so afraid that I don't think I can speak. I am sick with anger at myself for being so stupid. Marcus was in my head, Marcus with his shaved head and his scowl.

Jonah has cut the engines and the boat sits, water slapping against the sides. I know we are in the middle of the Sound, no land in sight. He goes to the sink, takes a washcloth, and wets it. He hands it to me.

"I'm sorry you got hurt," he says. "I'm not going to hurt you."

I press the washcloth against my lip.

"I'm going to save you," he says. "I'm going to give you a home."

He sits across the table from me. "Are you hungry? Thirsty?"

I don't answer.

"Your cell phone won't work," he says. "I have a blocker. A device that disrupts the signal. One of the advantages of being a techno-wizard." He smiles, but it dims when I don't respond. "It's just that I need a chance to talk to you," he says. "It takes time for you to understand, for you to see. I wasn't lying to you. I do have a foundation. It's just a little . . . unconventional, and I needed to get you away so you could really listen to me and not walk away. But if you want to leave, I'll take you back."

I seize on this, a tiny flame of hope. "I want to leave."

He smiles slightly. "But you haven't heard me yet."

This is crazy. It's like the guy is selling real estate.

He spreads his hands on the table and looks down at them. His fingers are long and slender. "People have it all wrong about families. Families don't work the way they are. All we hear about is 'family values, family values,' and I'm not even sure what that means. Loyalty? Love? Is that a blood connection or a value? Values aren't tied to blood. They're tied to brains. Everyday decisions that you make. That's values."

I'm trying to follow him, but it's hard. He's almost making sense, but not quite.

"So our families let us down, say. They demean us, or they desert us, or they just can't cope. There comes a point where you make your own family with your friends. But that doesn't work, either, because friendships have different boundaries. You don't share a life with your friends. You're not forced to live with them and deal with them. You can just walk away."

"I thought you had a happy childhood," I say.

He looks startled. "I did. Oh, I did. I'm talking about *other people*. I'm talking about the things I learned. Okay? Okay? Just *listen*."

There's perspiration on his forehead, and his eyes are damp. There is a flash of something in his eyes that frightens me.

I swallow against the knot of fear that rises in my throat. I put my hands under the table and squeeze them together. I will get through this. I will find a way out. I will find Emily. He didn't bring me out here to throw me overboard. I tell myself this very firmly. I don't know what's in store for me, but it isn't drowning. I will take this one step at a time. Diego knows where I am. He might have seen the boat take off. At the very least, he knows I was investigating Marcus and Ryan. The trail will lead to Jonah Castle eventually.

"I know what you're thinking," he interrupts.

"You can walk away from your family, too. But if you do, there's a *hole*. You fall into it, you can never climb out of it, it's just there. The problem is that people walk away from their family, but they don't replace it with something real. Okay?"

I nod, because it seems he needs encouragement.

"So I came up with this idea. We remake our family. We choose the people we want in it. And then we make a bond. Family values, okay? We support each other. We love each other. We're loyal."

"Like a commune?" I ask.

"No! Not like a commune!" He looks angrily at me, and the terror rises again.

"Like a real family," I say quickly. "Like the family you want, but thought you could never have."

"Exactly!" He looks eager now. "I have everything you need. You'll have brothers and sisters who will love you. I have a great house, and games, and books, and DVDs, and all the food you want, everything, everything! If you want to learn you can learn, if you want to play you can play, you can develop your specialness within this group that supports and loves you!" He leans forward. "Do you understand, Dora? I chose you!"

"What about Marcus?" I ask.

He waves a hand. "Marcus was useful, but not suitable. Too independent. But I told him I had this foundation, and he recommended kids he thought could benefit from internships and things . . ."

So Marcus had no idea what he was doing. He probably recommended Kendall, and then Emily. He never connected Kendall running away with Jonah Castle. And he might not even know that Emily is missing.

I've been wrong about everything. This kind of failure is colossal. It is beyond stupid. It is unforgivable.

But I know somehow I can't sink into the swamp of shame, because then I'll never get out, I'll never find Emily. I have a sudden instinct that hating myself will only help Jonah Castle.

"So where is your house?" I ask.

He springs up, happy. "You want to see it? It's solar-powered!"

"Where is it?" I ask.

"You'll see! You'll love it. Everyone does. I'm so glad you'll come over!"

He starts to spring up the steps.

"Jonah?"

He stops, looks at me.

"I'm not Dora," I say.

"I know," he says serenely, and continues up the stairs.

TWENTY-FIVE

The island is small, a gray smudge against the gray sea. Fog has rolled in, and gusts of wind send rolling slabs of it across the water. We have been traveling for hours. I don't wear a watch, and the fog obscures the sun, so I can't be sure, but it has to be at least three hours since we left Seattle.

"Come on up on deck!" Jonah yells down to me. "It's a beautiful sight!"

I climb up to the deck. Small droplets of mist hit my cheeks along with spray. A small boathouse looms ahead. I'm cold. It had been sunny in Seattle. I feel as though we are as far away as we can get, that we've passed beyond the boundary of the map and are in a gray wasteland of water that has yet to be discovered.

Jonah steers the boat into the boathouse and cuts the engine. He ties the lines and jumps up on deck, holding out a hand for me. I ignore him and jump onto the deck myself.

Nothing can dampen his enthusiasm. "Wait until you meet the others, Lizbet."

"What?"

"Come on." Jonah swipes a card through the

lock and opens the boathouse door for me to step through.

I walk out onto a beach. His eagerness seems eerie. Up beyond the beach is a high wall that crosses the beach and disappears into the trees. The door in the wall looks like steel. My footsteps crunch as I walk, and I realize I'm walking on oyster shells.

Sorry, Zed. I'll get out and clear you. I will.

He walks up to the wall and flips open a panel. He swipes a card, and the steel door opens.

Ahead, a long, low house hugs the ground. It's built of stone and wood, gray and brown, merging with the colors of the beach. It takes a moment for me to realize what is strange about it. The windows are sealed with metal shutters, like hurricane shutters.

My footsteps falter, and I am afraid.

I picture dead people inside the house, propped up like dolls.

The perspiration is gathering on my neck, under my arms, and I'm starting to shake uncontrollably.

He swipes the door frame with a card. A disembodied voice says, *Welcome home, Jonah.* The door swings open. He steps forward expectantly, happily.

The hallway floor is made of slabs of gray stone. There's a small bonsai tree on a graceful wood table to our right.

"Frances is our green thumb," he says.

He looks around. "It's activity time. Everyone's in the playroom. They'll all be dying to meet you."

Dying. I wish he hadn't used that word.

He swipes another keypad and pushes open the door directly in front of us. We step into the living area. It is a large open space scattered with three overstuffed sofas and at least a half-dozen big cushioned armchairs. The colors are the same as the island, bone, gray, black, dark green. Skylights let in a bit of light, and I can see the fog blowing overhead. The interior looks like a mountain cabin that's been blown up to three times its size. There is a large blank screen on one wall. DVDs and books line the shelves.

Emily is here. I can feel her now. She's close.

I get a flash of her, taking a book down from the shelves in this room.

She puts it back.

The repetition of the movement soothes her.

She does it again, sliding the book into the empty space.

"You see, Lizbet? Anything you want. You have it." He gestures toward the shelves. "All the latest movies. And TV, too! I select the programs, and you just have to scroll through the menu. This is where we have family time after supper."

"My name isn't Lizbet," I say.

"I know that," he says gently. "I'm not crazy."

"I'm not Dora, either."

He looks surprised. "What?"

"I'm Gracie."

He regards me for a moment, weighing something. "You belong," he says finally. "You still belong. I have an instinct about this stuff. Anyway, you'll want a new name to go with your new life soon. Names have associations."

"I don't want a new name."

He looks hurt. "Well, you don't have to."

He took away our names! Emily's voice screams in my head.

The house is so quiet. I don't even hear our footsteps.

"This is the site of the house I grew up in," Jonah says. "The same footprint, anyway. I loved that house and I tried to build a replica, but it was hard, you know. You can't build something exactly. Materials are harder to get, and, well, I had different needs. You can't blame me for modifying the design just a little bit. But it's essentially the same. I need to do it over again, okay? Nothing wrong with that. Anybody would say that, right?"

I blink. His words had started to echo. Suddenly, I see a different house. It's only a flash. The ceiling is low. There is a mattress on the floor with a baby on it. The baby is crying. A young boy sits nearby, reading, ignoring the baby.

Somewhere, another kid is screaming.

"And, of course, I had to wire it for digital controls. It's a smart house, do you know what that is?"

I shake my head, still reeling over my flash. Had I seen what is in Jonah's mind? Had I seen the reality of what it used to be? It was as though time was leaking inside me, forming a pool that contained present and past and future, and I had no control when I dipped into it what I would find.

"I can operate everything from one central panel," Jonah says. "Oven, generator, security, music, you name it. I control it, but you can ask me to do things. I mean, turn up the heat, whatever. The thing is, we have to accept the reality of the hierarchy. The hierarchy is good. The oldest takes care of the next oldest. And so on. And so that leaves me as the head of the house. So I make sure everyone is warm and fed and safe. I can do that. But we all take care of each other, too." He peers at me. "You understand? We all protect each other. That's the most important thing. That's what I learned about family. Here's where we eat. All together, of course, for the evening meal. That's fun, right?"

He pushes open double doors to a dining area. The table is long and can easily fit fourteen or more. There are benches instead of chairs, except at one of the ends, where a straight-backed wooden chair sits.

The room flashes again, and I see a smaller table, crowded with children. They sit on long benches on either side of the table. A man at the head, a thin man with a long beard. A woman at the other end, her eyes downcast. The children eating, silently, staring down at their plates.

I see the man's mouth move. A tall boy, thin as a pencil, looks up. He appears transfixed by his father's gaze. It is Jonah as a boy, I realize. I see the same blue eyes, but they are glassy with fear. I see that he is holding himself so still that his shoulders ache.

The dread at the table gathers. The other children continue to eat, continue to chew, but I can tell they aren't tasting their food. They are afraid to stop.

In a gesture stunning in its casualness, the man takes the boy's plate and sweeps it to the ground. The mother begins to run around the table to get it.

The father stops her.

Slowly, Jonah leans over to pick up the food.

"Meals are bonding time," Jonah is saying to me. I see him now, grown up, a man. I can't see the child behind his eyes. "I know, it's a cliché, bonding, right? But that's exactly what we do. Share our day and our food."

He hesitates. "There's only one rule. You have to stay inside the compound. That's what the wall is for. It's for your protection, you see. When I'm not here, I have to make sure you're safe. But that's not so bad, when there's so much to do inside our walls! I think traveling is overrated, don't you? Now. Let's meet the others."

He swipes a card and a door swings back. He waits impatiently for me to walk in, and I take baby steps, afraid of what I'll find.

It is a long room that ends in double doors at both ends. There are computers set up in different nooks. Sofas and chairs. More books and DVDs. Huge screens fill the walls, projecting images of nature. One whole wall is made up of a waterfall. The waterfall I'd seen in my vision. No wonder it hadn't seemed right. It had been a projection. The room is unnaturally bright, track lights on the ceiling mimicking a sunny day. It's so normal it's spooky.

There are kids here, dressed in jeans and sweatpants and T-shirts. None of them is talking to one another or working together. That's what's so strange — the silence. They are in their separate niches. One girl is potting a plant. One is playing with a Game Boy. A boy is reading a book. The rest are at computers. My gaze roams restlessly, anxiously, searching for Emily.

I spot her in a corner, at a computer, staring at the screen, and my heart leaps. At least I have found her. At least I have done that. And she is alive, and looks okay. Relief warms me instantly.

Jonah follows my gaze, then walks over, and I follow. She glances up furtively, then hunches her shoulders. In that quick glance, I try to convey to her to not reveal that we know each other. I'm not sure if she gets it. All I can see in her gaze is blankness.

Alarm clangs inside me.

This is not the Emily I know.

This is the Emily I sensed.

The one who wants to disappear inside herself so she can escape the fear.

"That's our Nell, always working."

He touches her, and I can see how she shrinks against the touch of his fingers, long and supple, on her shoulder.

She hates and fears him.

He singles her out. The pressure of that is too much for her.

It is crushing her.

Jonah turns away and takes my arm to bring me to the center of the room. "Meet your brothers and sisters." There is just the hint of an eye roll from a girl slouched on a sofa, watching TV. She had once been a blond, but now black roots extended three inches into her hair.

Jonah whistles through his teeth. "New member of the family has arrived. Do you remember the procedure?"

Suddenly, the kids move. Even the black-rooted surly girl on the sofa snaps to. They line up, ten girls and boys. Emily is four down from the top. I feel completely surreal, like I'm Maria the nun and Jonah is Captain Von Trapp in *The Sound of Music*.

As he calls out the names, each girl or boy raises a hand. It is amazing how much they give away by this simple gesture.

"Susannah." Barely raises her fingers, pushing insolence as far as she dares for me.

"Edwin." Blond boy, Susannah's height, jerks hand up, giving me an assessing stare.

"Frances. Our songbird." Frances nods tentatively. Inside my head, I hear a name. *Kendall*. This is Kendall Farmer.

"Tate." Eyes on the ground, nervously lifts hand, bad skin, emotional disturbance he wears like a coat.

"Nell." Emily lifts her hand quickly, then drops it, not looking at us.

"Hank and Dan, the twins." Two boys looking nothing alike, raise their hands. They hate each other.

And then the flash comes again. Instead of Jonah, I see his father. In a dim, dark room, children are lined up on their knees. I see the bearded man mouth the names as Jonah does.

". . . Ruthanna, Maudie, Eli."

The twelve children are lined up in a row, oldest to youngest. Fear rises off their bodies like steam. None of them look at their father. As they rise, one of them — maybe it's Edwin, one of the older children — winces in pain, as though the act of rising hurt him. I think again about the boy I heard screaming in my vision.

And I'm back in the present, in the brightly lit room.

The two youngest, Maudie and Eli, have already started to eye the computers they've left.

Jonah spreads his arms. "Family."

The expressions on the faces of the kids tell me nothing except they want this over with.

I look at Eli, maybe eleven years old, but small and pale. He comes out of foster care. I see the house, crowded with kids. Foster parents who do it for the money. I see Eli sitting in a closet, making his own space there. He has a ball. He has three crayons.

Jonah continues. "Let's see, Lizbet is between Frances and Nell, so Frances, show Lizbet her bed and help her feel at home. I think she needs a sweatshirt; it was a cold ride. I'll see you all at supper." Jonah heads for the door.

I stand in the middle of the room in disbelief.

What now? The other kids drift away, but the girl and boy he called Susannah and Edwin come closer, close enough so that we are almost touching.

"That this group must somehow form a family," Edwin sings in my ear. He manages to make it sound nasty, threatening.

"Forget the names. I'm Torie," the girl says. "This is Jeff. Castle won't hurt you if you listen to us."

"Just do what he says," Jeff says. "And what we say, too. Then you'll be okay."

I look around at the other kids, who are deliberately ignoring me. They are afraid of Torie and Jeff. They are locked in their isolation. This isn't even close to the family ideal Jonah wants.

I know now why Emily has closed down. Nobody is leaving. Nobody is getting out of here.

There is no hope left in this room.

TWENTY-SIX

Frances-Kendall shows me the layout. The bedrooms are at both ends of the long room. The girls all sleep together in beds lined up like a dormitory. There are no windows, but there is a projection of a Webcam shot of the Sound.

"He checks on us," she says. "Sometimes five times a night. With a flashlight. So be here."

I remember the light in my vision, sweeping the bed, Emily shrinking from it, pretending to be asleep. The darkness, and then the light. I hadn't seen a lighthouse at all.

"If you're awake, he hates it," she says.

"Thank you, Kendall," I say.

She starts. "How did you know my name?"

"Your parents miss you," I say. "They found a girl who looks like you in San Diego, but it wasn't you, and they were crushed."

She works her mouth, sucking in her lip, biting it, letting it out. "Don't talk to me about my parents. Don't ever talk to me about them again," she hisses, and walks away.

★   ★   ★

Dinner. We line up on benches. Jonah has a chair. The girls had prepared the meal, me included. Jonah had brought fresh supplies from Seattle, and I recognize some of the stores, thanks to Shay. Fresh ravioli. Big loaves of bread from a designer bakery in Ballard. A chunk of parmesan that we grate over the ravioli. Bags of green beans so fresh they snap. It's easy for four of us to make the meal because the kitchen is huge. There are two ovens and a professional stove and every size pot you could want.

I think of how Shay would love this kitchen and feel something so new I can't identify it at first. I'm homesick.

Jonah takes a bite and pronounces it delicious. We all start to eat.

"We're finally all together," he says, looking around. "Now that Lizbet has joined us, the family is complete. Lizbet is our poet. Nell is our soul. Just like Frances is our voice, or Ruthanna makes us laugh."

Ruthanna keeps looking down at her plate and shoveling in ravioli. A less likely candidate for a laugh I've never seen. She's probably about thirteen. She doesn't meet anyone's eyes.

I see her suddenly, in the backseat of a black car, pulling away down a road. She's younger. I see gravestones behind her. Her mother is dead, but she can't understand why they're leaving her. I can feel her grief as keenly as I can feel mine.

She doesn't care what happens to her here. She is glad that the food is good.

Jonah smiles. His sleeves are rolled up, and he looks like any dad at a kitchen table.

"This is what my father believed, and I believe it, too," he says, and I realize that he's directing his remarks to me. "That the family can be a self-sufficient unit. Each of you has your own skill. We can entertain each other. We have artists and musicians and scientists here."

This gives me my opening. I need to unsettle him. I need to see what happens when I do.

"What we need is a cook," I say.

The rest of the kids freeze. Jonah blinks at me, as if my words are taking a long time to register.

He smiles tightly. "There is something wrong with the food?"

Torie gives me a murderous look.

"Well," I say, "it could be better."

His smile wobbles, then freezes. "I got this ravioli from the best place in Seattle."

"Really." I poke at my dish. "It tastes like glue."

Across the table, Torie mouths something at me. *You die.*

Jonah stands up. He is shaking with fury. Emily closes her eyes. "I bring you the best! I take care of you! You know that, Lizbet!" he shouts, his face red.

"My name is Gracie," I say.

"I know that!" he snaps. "Everyone else likes their new names!"

Torie gets up quickly. She removes my plate and takes it to the kitchen. As she moves, she jabs against me, hard, with her elbow.

Jonah's hand grips his fork. "Well. Supper is not about food. It is about communication and love. We love each other."

"We love each other," Jeff echoes. He shoots me a look that eloquently says, *shut up, idiot.*

Kendall bites her lip and pushes her food around. She is afraid and wants me to stop. She casts a quick look at Jeff, then looks away.

She's afraid of Jonah, yes. But she's also afraid of Torie and Jeff.

"Yes, Edwin. Let's eat." Jonah takes a bite of his dinner. Everyone starts to eat again.

I take a sip of my water. When Jonah stood up, I noticed something. In his front left pocket, I saw the tip of his swipe card. Of course, he probably keeps it on him at all times. The card works on the locks, but didn't he also say that he can control everything? Music, heating, security. There has to be a central control. It has to be in his wing of the house.

"This is all new to you," Jonah says suddenly, turning to me. His anger is gone. "You'll understand things in time. I was too harsh. I'm never harsh."

I see his father standing over a young Jonah, shouting, *This is what I do for you! I do this for you! Do you understand?*

"You do this for me," I say.

He shakes his head rapidly as if shaking out a mop full of dust. "Exactly."

I smell smoke suddenly. It is acrid, strong. Yet I don't cough, it doesn't fill my lungs, and I can't see it in the air. I look around, but everyone else is eating.

"I do this for all of you," Jonah mumbles.

I realize that the smoke is not in the air. It's in my head. And for the first time I wonder — what happened to the original house?

Jonah said that now we were complete. What came next? There was an end to this, and the only one who knows the ending is Jonah.

TWENTY-SEVEN

I wake up in the middle of the night. I hear the even breathing of the other girls. Jonah could come by at any time; I know he's already checked us at least once. His visits are random, so there is no way to avoid them.

But I can't wait any longer. I'll have to take a chance.

I slip out of bed. Emily's bed is right next to mine. I put my hand over her mouth. She tries to bolt up, terror in her eyes, but I speak quietly, rapidly, in her ear.

"It's Gracie. Don't worry. I just want to talk to you."

She shakes her head, her eyes fearful.

"Just for a minute."

"He'll come."

"I'm going to get you out of here."

She shakes her head. "No. Don't say that. It's dangerous."

"Why? Has he done anything to you?"

She turns away. "No, nothing. It's just that . . . he pays attention to me. Special attention. He watches me, all the time."

"I came to find you, Emily. Your mom, your dad . . . they're frantic. They miss you."

Emily starts to cry. I feel her shudders as she tries to keep her sobs inside. I'm actually glad to see her cry. It's so much better than that blankness.

"It's okay," I say, even though it's so obviously not.

I can see tears on her cheeks from the light cast from the watery reflection on the wall. "I'm glad you're here. But Gracie . . ."

"What?"

"Don't do it. Don't try to get away. Promise me." Her eyes are frantic.

"Shhh," I say, as if Emily were a little girl. "Go back to sleep."

Torie approaches me the next morning as I'm looking through the bookshelves. I can't imagine having enough concentration to read, but I don't know what else to do.

She stands a little too close for my personal comfort.

"Maybe I didn't make myself clear," she says. "Keep your mouth shut and you'll do okay here."

I shrug. Her gaze is so hostile. Why should I give her ammunition?

Her face is in my face. "Don't say your real name to him," she warns, spitting the words out. "Don't *ever* do it again."

Just what I need — to get snatched by a madman and then get bossed around by another girl. "Look," I say, exasperated, "I've been kidnapped by a psycho who makes up crazy rules according to some insane scenario in his head. I've got enough problems without having to listen to you, too. Don't you want to get out of here?"

"Listen up," she says. "This is a sweet spot compared to where I came from. Most of us here are the same. This is *better* than home. You're not going to take it away from us. One of these days, I'll figure out a way to leave, but until then, I have everything I want here. Just what do you want to send us back to? Our families?" She snorts. "The streets? Keep quiet and don't make him crack up."

I'm listening, but I'm also seeing her. Smoking a cigarette on a street corner. Crouching down in the cold. She had been homeless.

I see that things that have happened to her have made her capable of anything. Kendall is right to be afraid of her.

But I also know one thing. I can't show her my fear. "And what do you think will happen if he *does* crack up?" I ask. "It's scary inside his head."

"It's scary inside *my* head. Don't forget that."

I see a man, sitting in an armchair, smiling up at Torie. Her hair is shorter and blonder. Her smile is strained. He reaches up and, with his foot, rubs her leg.

The vision derails me for a moment.

"Look," I say to her, "There's no telling what he could do to us."

Torie snorts. "He's a millionaire. He's famous. What's he going to do?"

"He's kidnapped kids," I say. I can't believe that she is this stupid. "He committed about a thousand felonies. They can put him away for life. Do you know what that means? He has nothing left to lose."

Torie looks at me as though I'm the one who's stupid. "Rich people don't go to prison. Don't you know that?"

Jonah approaches us, his hands in his pockets, smiling. "I'm glad to see you're getting along already." He looks at me. "You know, there's a garden. We all planted it. Tomatoes, herbs, lettuce."

I don't know what he expects me to say, so I say the conventional thing. "That's nice."

"So we have fresh produce sometimes," he says. "I just wanted you to know that. Sometimes I overreact. That doesn't mean I don't love you."

A small boy lies in a bed, crying.

Sometimes I hurt you. That doesn't mean I don't love you. When you do bad things, that hurts me, too. But you still love me, right, Jonah?

"When I do bad things, that hurts you, too," I say.

Jonah blinks. "Exactly," he says. "Come and help me pick lettuce."

I follow Jonah out the kitchen door. It's good to be outside. The fog has lifted, and it's a bright summer day, warm enough to be in a T-shirt. I could almost feel hopeful on a day like this. If I weren't stuck on an island in the middle of nowhere with no way to get off.

Still, the sun is warm on the skin of my arms and my face, and it drains some of the anxiety from my muscles. We walk along the back of the house, and Jonah strikes off on a path between the trees. From here, you can't see the wall. Strangely, I am not afraid to be alone with him. Not now, anyway. Somehow I know he won't hurt me . . . at least, not yet.

"The garden is this way. I sited it so that it gets the most sun. Had to truck in some super-duper soil. You know, Lizbet was the sister I was closest to." He says this last part quickly, running into the discussion about topsoil, stripped of any emotion, just matter-of-fact.

"I mean, Nell was the special one. The rest of us . . . we didn't protect each other. We told on each other, as a matter of fact. But we all protected Nell. I was closest to Lizbet, though."

"Where is Lizbet now?"

"My father wasn't a monster." Jonah stops. We are in the middle of a glade, and it's cooler here. He picks up a pine branch and begins to strip the needles. "I don't want you to think that. He and my mother left San Francisco because they didn't like the atmosphere there. Everyone thought they were weird for having twelve kids. So they moved to the foothills of the Sierras for a while. I remember that. I was ten when we moved here. He said the family was the core of society, and if we made the perfect family, we could show the world how to live. He really believed that. Perfection was everything to him. He encouraged all of us to reach our potential. He shipped in my computer stuff. It wasn't like he didn't want us to succeed. He just wanted us to be special."

"Is your dad still alive?" I ask.

He looks around vaguely. He scratches his arm with the tree branch. His skin is pale, as if he never goes outside in the summer. He has a face people wouldn't remember. He's not handsome, but he's not bad-looking. There's no distinguishing feature in his face. Everything is in proportion, everything makes sense. But his eyes don't focus on the world.

"I don't see any of them now," he says.

Jonah is speaking to me now as an adult. I realize that this is why I felt such a disconnect with him. I remember him on the boat. *It's solar-powered! I'm glad you can come over!* Sometimes he speaks like a teenager. And sometimes he speaks like he is, like a man. He slips from one to the other.

"I just want you to have a nice meal," he says to me, with such simple directness I suddenly wonder if I'm the one who's crazy, and he's completely sane.

"You said you'd bring me back if I didn't want to stay." I figure I can at least try this when he seems so reasonable.

He cocks his head and smiles. "But you haven't given us a chance."

"I'm not Dora," I tell him. "I don't have an alcoholic mother. I'm not looking to be saved."

He nods. "But you belong here anyway. Don't you?" He takes a step closer to me, and I step back. "There's a hole in you," he says. He touches my collarbone, and I try to control my instinct, which is to shudder. But the touch is light and fleeting. "Here. Inside you. I can see it. You're like me. All of you, you're all like me."

"There's a lot of pain here," I say.

"That's why this will work. All it takes is time."

He starts walking again, and I follow as if tethered to him on a string. We break through the trees into a clearing.

The garden hasn't been weeded or watered. Some of the tomatoes have fallen off the vine and lie on the ground, split and rotten. Flies buzz over the pulp. Jonah stands, hands on his hips, looking at it. He begins to slap his thigh rhythmically.

"They were supposed to take care of this."

"It's not so bad," I say.

"We're all supposed to work together for each other."

"There's some nice tomatoes left."

"We're supposed to *help* each other."

His voice is strained and cracking. He is slapping his thigh harder now, slapping it with the branch he still holds in his hand. I start to back up.

"We're supposed to work *together*!" he screams. "How is this going to work if they don't *listen*! It's all their fault, and they won't try hard enough, and it's all about that, isn't it? We have to share. If only they could see that. How much harder can I try? They make me sick, they make me so mad!"

I have heard this voice before. I have heard this rant in my vision. I have seen this dark energy spill over in a torrent, and it is scarier in person.

He throws down the branch and picks up the hoe. He begins to hack at the garden, the tomato plants, the lettuces, the herbs, slamming the hoe into the ground, into the plants, over and over. Tears are running down his face. The hoe is flying in the air, a weapon now.

The rage came on so fast. How could I have not realized how dangerous he was? The danger was there, beneath the surface, beneath the khakis and the glasses and the smile.

I turn and run. I run through the forest, afraid

he is following me, but I am alone with the whispering trees. I hear my breathing, frantic, and my footsteps on the hard ground. My footsteps pound out what I already know:

I have to find a way out.

TWENTY-EIGHT

I run straight into Jeff. Literally. I bounce off him and fall.

"Where's the fire?" he says.

The fire . . . the fire! I *see* it then, I see the house burning. But is it in the past, or the future?

I can't tell.

"What's the matter with you?" he asks, crouching over me.

"He went crazy," I say. "In the garden. He's destroying it. You didn't take care of it while he was away."

Jeff shrugs. "It's hard to remember everything he wants us to do."

"You don't understand. He's out of control!"

"He gets like that." Jeff pulls me to my feet. "Then he sort of shuts down for a while and disappears into the woods. That's the good part. I think he's afraid he'll hurt us."

"But what if he *does*?"

His face hardens. "I'm not afraid of him."

"Why don't we all just jump him? Take that swipe card — I saw it in his pocket. We can get to the boat —"

"Shut up," he says.

"We can get out of here!"

"Shut up," he says. His gaze is flat and hard. "Shut your mouth and keep it shut and follow the rules. You don't know crap. We're in the middle of nowhere, man. We've got it good here."

"You're just as crazy as he is." I try to push around him, but he grabs me by the upper arm.

"I've lived in a lot of places," he says. His grip is tight. "My dad is an addict. So I get bounced around every time he's in rehab. Or jail. Jonah is a meal ticket, and this is five-star dining. Got it?"

"I've got news for you," I say. "You're the one who's in jail."

His face tightens. "He's not around all the time. When he's not, Torie and I are in charge. I'd think about that, if I were you." He squeezes my arm until it hurts, and then he keeps on squeezing. I try to twist away, but it just hurts more.

Finally, he drops my arm, but he keeps his eyes on my face. I'm trembling, and my arm is on fire. I walk past him, trying not to run.

Inside, I stop in the kitchen and splash water on my face. I take deep breaths, trying to get my focus back. Jeff's words return.

Then he sort of shuts down and disappears into the woods. . . .

He's out there now, roaming in the woods, trying to get his control back. It's now or never. I have to try it when Jonah is here, because if I can get out of the house and past the wall, I'll need the boat. I can't rescue everyone, but I can get Emily and maybe Kendall. Once we get to the police, they can save the rest.

For a second, I waver. I think of pudgy Ruthanna at the dinner table, shoveling ravioli into her mouth. There is a sadness in her that is total. And Eli, and Maudie. They're only eleven or twelve. How can I leave them?

I have to leave them. It's the only way to get out of here. It's the only way to save them.

There are no sharp knives in the kitchen, only butter knives, but I take one, along with a fork.

The other wing of the house is Jonah's. It's separated from the rest of the house down a long hallway. The door is locked, of course. I kneel, examining the lock, but I don't know why. I don't know anything about lock-breaking. I try to stick the blade of the knife in between the door and the lock. I push and push. Nothing.

A shadow looms behind me and my heart leaps into my throat.

"If you open it, an alarm will go off. The place is wired."

It's Hank, one of the twins who aren't twins.

I slump against the door. "Oh."

He's eating a carrot stick. He waves it at the door. "You'll never be able to break the lock that way, anyway. You can't use a butter knife to break a lock."

"You know this?"

"I'm handy. My dad is a carpenter."

The words cause him pain. I see a man in a room. Sitting in a chair. Dogs surround him, licking at empty bowls.

Hank shakes off the emotion. He crunches into the carrot. "Anyway, I've been in there. He needed help once, there was a busted pipe in his bathroom and he couldn't fix it by himself. He needed someone with small hands. I'm good with my hands. There's a control panel in his bedroom. I saw it. But you need his swipe card to get inside. There's controls for everything. The shutters, the main power switch. There's a generator and a backup generator. The swipe cards work on batteries, so even if the power goes out, the doors stay locked unless he opens them. He's thought of everything. Even if you got in that room, there's nothing you could do."

"There's got to be something. A phone . . ."

"He doesn't bring his cell inside. He keeps it in the boat."

"The wall . . ."

"It's electrified, didn't he tell you?"

"So help me break into the room, and we'll turn off the power."

Slowly, he shakes his head. "I'm not rocking the boat."

"I don't understand," I say. "I don't understand any of you."

"That must be because you come from a place you want to get back to," Hank says. He shrugs.

"What about the other kids?" I ask. "What about the young ones, like Eli and Maudie? Don't they deserve better than this?"

Hank pops the rest of the carrot in his mouth. "Don't you get it? We're all in this alone."

He hears a noise and he freezes in fear for a moment. It is the back door opening. Jeff coming back, maybe. I don't care. But Hank does, and he quickly and silently moves down the hall.

I lean against the door for a moment. I have felt pain before that made me rock and howl. And I have felt trapped in a deep hole of sorrow with no way out. But this is different. This is horror wrapped in a normal package. This is knowing that the worst isn't behind me. The worst is ahead.

And I'm the only one who cares.

TWENTY-NINE

That night it rains, a hard, steady rain that drums on the roof insistently. We eat our meat loaf in silence. Jonah is distracted, as though he is listening to voices from far away.

He is.

Every so often his fork drops to his plate with a clink, and he sits, staring into nowhere.

Torie and Jeff glare at all of us, keeping us in line. The threat of violence hangs over us, impossible to misinterpret. I'm not sure what they'd do, but I'm sure they'd do it. They are the most desperate of all of us. They've lived on the streets. They want this safe berth. They want the food, and the clothes, and the warm bed. For them, this place *is* their future. The only future they can see. It was no accident that Torie had mentioned Jonah's money right away to me. She would do anything to protect her status here.

Torie directs us to clear the table, moves us with shoves when Jonah isn't looking. Everyone is quieter tonight. They move fast and efficiently. Jeff hovers over us in the kitchen, watching us put food away, stick the dishes in the dishwasher. Jonah stays at the table.

As we're getting ready for bed, Kendall whispers to me, "He doesn't like the rain."

"Whoa, is he living in the wrong part of the country," I say.

She twists her mouth as if it's been so long since she smiled that she doesn't remember how.

We all go to bed, and the house is silent except for the clamor of rain. When I see the flashlight, I freeze. I'm remembering Jonah outside in the garden, slashing at the plants, the sharp edge of the hoe coming down and scoring the earth. But I slip out of bed. The flashlight tracks me as I move toward him.

"Go back to bed," he says. He looks glassy-eyed, and he's perspiring. His hair is matted to his forehead.

"I'm afraid of the rain," I say.

His gaze doesn't stop; it just keeps roaming.

"I needed to check on Nell. Is Nell all right?"

"She's fine," I say. The light rests on Emily. I know she is awake, but her eyes are closed. She has drawn herself up into a tight little ball underneath the covers.

"Go to sleep," he says to me, but there is no force behind his words. He's not aware of me, really. He's looking at Emily.

He looks with a hunger that frightens me. He looks capable of anything.

I sag with relief when he turns and leaves the room. What I want is to crawl back into bed.

What I do is follow him.

He passes through the dark playroom and into the living area. He sits on the couch and takes off his glasses. His head falls into his hands. I don't say anything. I don't try to hide. I stand in the darkness, watching him.

"My head hurts," he moans.

There is a flash, but it isn't lightning, it's another vision. I am so open to them now, it's like the boat locks in Seattle, the water rushing in, filling the compartment, and everything rising with it. Only here, it is the past. I think it is because Jonah lives with the past. I can pick it up so easily from him.

It is Nell, I see now.

Nell is sick, very sick.

The father stands in the doorway. He won't let the mother go in.

I can hear the voices, but nobody's mouth moves.

They are frozen like statues.

The human body is perfect, I hear. It is Jonah's voice. I am hearing the memory through Jonah. *She has received the right caloric input, the correct balance of nutrients. Her body will fight this without our help.*

The mother is crying silently. Her hands are tightly clasped, as if she thinks that by taking on the posture of begging but not speaking, he will somehow listen to her.

Jonah stands behind them, the oldest boy.

Father. Dad. We can use the radio.

She needs no help.

He closes the door.

The vision fades.

"You wanted to help her," I say to Jonah.

His head is still in his hands. "I wanted to."

"You wanted to call for help on the radio."

"I did want to!" He raises his head, and his face is streaked with tears. His pale skin is wet and glows in the darkness. I can smell him now. He is sweating. "I sneaked in to see her. She was so sick."

I see him again. It is Nell he is carrying in the rain.

He didn't kill her.

She was already dead.

"You tried to get help," I say. "You tried to get her to the boat."

"I thought . . . if I could get her to the mainland. To a hospital."

"It wasn't your fault she died, Jonah."

"It was her birthday. She was thirteen. She was excited about that. About being a teenager. Being one of the older ones. Every birthday we thought, I am closer to getting out."

He curls up in a ball, resting his head on his elbow. "You know how when someone you love dies? It's like running into a wall. You bang your fists against it because you can't believe it's *real*. You can't believe you won't see that face again. You can't believe you won't hear that voice. You *can't believe* it."

"I know," I say. I swallow against a throat suddenly dry.

He looks up at me without moving. "You do know." In the dim light, I can see only the gleam of his eyes.

"Tell me," he says, and I know immediately what he wants me to say.

It is like the storm outside is inside me, and if I open my mouth it will rush out in a flood. This is the moment, this is it, this is the time when I *must* say it, crazily enough, on this nowhere island, to this crazy man full of pain.

I open my mouth. I feel something crack inside me like ice. Then the words come. "My mother is dead."

"How?"

"A car crash. She got caught between a semi and a truck. The truck was carrying oranges."

I can taste it suddenly, orange in my mouth. Jonah rises to a sitting position, his eyes on my face, not leaving. I have never felt so listened to before. He is listening with his whole body. He is eager to hear. He wants to fill up on my pain, he wants to know it. He wants to share it.

No, he doesn't want to share it.

He wants to take it for himself. He wants to *own* it.

And I want to give it away.

"The oranges rolled all over the road. She was . . . she was choking to death. On her blood. The oranges . . . I can't see it. But I *smell* it. I smell it sometimes. I *taste* it. I can't eat oranges. I can't even smell them. The smell makes me sick."

My mouth still open, I start to cry. The tears run into my open mouth. I collapse on the couch across the room from him. My sobs are so strong they wrench my belly. I reach for a pillow and grab it, slam it on my knees and push my face into it to cry. I've done this before. I know what to do with this kind of tears.

I thought this kind of crying was over.

It will never be over.

I almost feel a kinship with him now. Jonah knows that the grief that marks you never leaves. What haunts you, haunts you. Just when you think it lets go, it comes back with teeth and claws.

"I asked her not to go," I say into the pillow.

"You couldn't have stopped her."

"That's what people say. But they don't know. I could have."

I lift my head. The pillow is wet. I am lying in a stain of my own tears.

I look at the damaged man across the room. I want to say, *I am damaged, too.*

I don't have to. He already knows it.

He crawls over to me. He lifts my chin so that we are at eye level. His gaze is tender.

Now I smell the burning again, and this time I see the house on fire and the children running. A window blows out, the glass flying into the night air.

His face is close. His eyes unfocus. His whisper is anguished and hushed and for my ears alone. "I don't want to do it, Lizbet. Help me."

THIRTY

Torie finds me the next morning as I'm brushing my teeth at the row of three sinks in the girls' bathroom. Kendall is next to me, washing her face. Ruthanna is just putting her toothbrush away.

"Hey," Torie says. "I saw you. Last night."

I shrug, brush, and spit. I'm leaning over the sink when she puts her hand on the back of my head and grabs my hair. She pushes me down hard. My teeth clunk against the faucet. I feel the impact shudder into the root.

"Oh, good," she says. "I have your attention."

Kendall backs up quickly, but hovers in the doorway. Ruthanna just vanishes.

Torie keeps my head against the faucet. She is amazingly strong. I have a feeling that if I try to resist, I'll lose my front teeth.

She leans over, close to my ear. "I was the first," she says, her words like bullets. Occasionally, for emphasis, she pushes me against the sink faucet. Not hard, just a bump, but it's enough. My lip is still healing from falling down the stairs on the boat, and every time it hits the chrome I wince.

"He found me first. I'm closest to him. I'm the

one he depends on. So don't think you can come here and work it."

"Hey, list —"

Bang. My face hits the faucet.

"Because I'm drawing the line."

Torie's words overlap with someone else's. I flash suddenly to a blond woman, tan and thin, well muscled, perfectly groomed. I hear a voice echo. "I know your tricks. I've never drawn the line enough with you. Now I'm drawing the line."

Torie leans in. "Let me remind you of something, *Lizbet*. You've already disappeared. Nobody's going to know if you do it again."

But I can't avoid him. Something has changed between us. He watches Emily, but he talks to me. He singles me out. He directs remarks to me. He asks me how I like the macaroni and cheese. He offers to order new DVDs.

He likes me.

I can feel Torie's and Jeff's eyes on me. I know they are wondering how to handle me. I know that they will not handle me with kid gloves. I am heading to a cliff and I don't know who's going to push me off.

He comes and gets me now, in the middle of the night. I follow him like a ghost in my T-shirt and Gap sweatpants, what we all sleep in. We are both barefoot. His feet are long and white and feminine-looking. It makes him seem fragile, even though I know he's not. He sits on the couch with his head in his hands. Sometimes he cries.

"I can't sleep," he says.

I get flashes, but they are confusing. I see him as a boy, running, breathing hard, barefoot on the oyster shells on the beach. I know someone is chasing him.

I see Nell, lying on the bed. I know she is dead. She is wet with rain. The wetness pools out on the sheets.

I'm tired during the day, from the nights spent with Jonah. And I'm holding on to what I can see and what I can touch, because I keep sliding into places that the kids hide deep inside their minds, places they don't want to go.

But they go all the time.

Eli. His older foster brother tied him up and flicked matches at him. For fun.

Maudie. Is clumsy. That's what her mother tells the doctor.

Ruthanna. Her mother died, and it was her fault. Her father told her so.

Dan. His father left him at his grandmother's to play one day. Never came back.

Hank. His father drinks. His mother works

two shifts. His brother died last year. He spends all his time alone.

Tate . . .

I am afraid of what's in Tate's head.

There is just too much pain in this house.

I can feel it. I can *see* it.

Everything parents can do, the world can do, to mess up a kid — it's all here. It lives in their heads.

They feel safe here because they don't know what safe is. This, they figure, is as close as they'll get.

He tells me about Nell. That from the first, she was the one they protected. That there was something special about her. Out of all of them, she was the one they all loved.

When she got sick, the fragile bonds fell apart. The family disintegrated. The panic was a string that vibrated at a pitch they could all hear. The children walked around with dread, fearing the inevitable. Fearing that what they knew would happen would happen: Their father would not give in.

"I can remember better when you're around," he says. "You help me remember." It's two o'clock in the morning. He is lying on one couch; I am lying on another.

"That's good," I say, trying not to yawn.

"I don't want to remember," he says.

"I'm sorry." A trickle of fear begins inside me. I feel him trying to push something away in his mind, something huge.

This is the thing he's blocked from me.

This is the thing he's blocked from himself.

"Her birthday is on Friday, you know. The birthday she never had. That's when it has to happen."

"What has to happen?"

"He was afraid it would all fall apart, that they would think he wasn't fit."

I smell burning. I smell the fire.

"He was afraid they'd take us away. He tried to save us."

I see the glass shatter, fall into blackness. I hear someone pounding on a door.

"I don't want to do it," Jonah says. "But I have to save us, too."

Friday. I try to remember what day it is.

I look out into the darkness. He is just a shape across the room. What he's saying doesn't make sense to me, but it doesn't have to. It makes sense to him.

There is urgency in his mind now. He is racing toward a goal. He has given up controlling this. He has given up analyzing it. He has given up changing it.

Whatever he is heading for, in his mind, he will have saved us. In his mind, he'll be able to rest.

Tomorrow is Thursday. I have to gather all the hazy ideas, the things I know, the things I guess, the things I'm thinking, and make a plan.

I only have one day to set it up.

One day to make it work.

THIRTY-ONE

The next morning, I find Emily in the laundry room, folding socks. There are two machines, two dryers, drying racks, a row of detergents and softeners. He makes it as easy as he can.

Emily has a row of white socks lined up. She is concentrating hard, as though it is the most difficult thing in the world to match up white socks. She smooths each sock as she places it on the long table used for folding.

"Emily," I say. "Are you okay?"

She isn't really here. I can feel that her focus on the socks is absolute. She likes the repetition of the motion, the smell of the bleach. She likes how white they are.

I put my hand over hers to stop her movement. She slips it out and keeps going.

"Do you know what I was afraid of when I was little?" she says, looking down at the socks. "Not monsters, or earthquakes. Infinity."

"Infinity?"

"I was in Sunday school. They taught us that in heaven, you just keep going on. Before I went to sleep, I'd think about that. I'd try to imagine going on and on, never being able to stop. I tried to imagine something never ending. And it used to terrify me. I'd run and get into my parents' bed. Dad would ask me what was wrong, and I'd say I was afraid of monsters, or the lion at the zoo. Whatever. I thought it was too weird to tell him that I was afraid of infinity."

She smoothes another sock, places one on top of it.

"Emily, we're all in danger. We have to get out of here."

She smoothes another sock.

"Emily, I'm thinking of a way. But it won't work if we all can't do it together."

She begins to hum.

"I need your help. We have to face this!"

"This isn't like you," she says primly. She takes another sock and rolls it up like a bandage.

"What are you talking about?"

"Nothing bothers you," she says. "You're a closed system."

She isn't making sense, and I'm scared. I watch her fold socks. And then the truth crashes down on my head so dizzily I want to fall on the floor and grab onto the floor to keep myself steady.

I had never asked myself the questions that were staring me in the face about our friendship. Why did Emily drop the friends she'd known all her life, the girls who'd known her since kindergarten, the boys who knew her parents, the group that hung together through long Saturday afternoons, through endless rainy February weeks, through crushes, through bad teachers, through pizza on Fridays?

Why had she picked me? It certainly wasn't because I was such a fun companion. It wasn't because we could share our sorrows.

It was because she knew that I wouldn't make her feel.

I would never ask her things. I would never push her. I would never make her cry.

She knew, with the cunning of the wounded, that I couldn't turn away from myself long enough to even *see* her. She could slowly close herself off. And no one would knock on the door.

Her abduction by Jonah was an example of the worst possible thing happening to her at the worst possible time. She had already begun to disengage. Now she was filling up her head with distance. And soon, no one would be able to reach her.

I'm still shaken by my encounter with Emily, but I'm more determined than ever to follow through on the plan that's forming in my mind. Kendall and I have the lunch dishes to do. She washes; I dry. We are only allowed to use the dishwasher at night. Too much power can blow the generator.

"I think we have a friend in common," I say. "Marcus Heffernan."

"Marcus?" Kendall looks surprised.

"He worked at the computer camp. I went there looking for Emily. She's met him, too."

"I've never really talked to Nell . . . Emily." Kendall smiles, sort of dreamily, and the muscles in her face relax. For the first time, I realize that she could be pretty. "I had a big crush on Marcus. He was so nice to me."

"You sang in that café he works in."

"Did he tell you about that? He talked me into entering that contest. I was so nervous, I thought I would die. And then I won second prize! That was a good day." Kendall puts away a dish. "Which was not the usual."

"You had a hard time with your parents."

"Yeah. How about you?"

"My mom is dead. I never really knew my dad."

"Oh. Yeah. Well."

A rather pathetic attempt at sympathy, but never mind.

"Have you ever seen Jonah have a meltdown?" I ask her, handing her a dish.

She looks around before answering me. "Yeah."

"Scary, huh?"

She doesn't answer.

She doesn't have to.

She reaches up to replace the dish on a shelf.

"Did you know that the original house burned down?" I ask.

"No." She takes a dish, glances at me, then back down at the dish.

"The children were trapped inside."

She doesn't look up, but the dish is dry, and she keeps rubbing.

"Don't you wonder what Jonah is trying to make up for?"

"It's none of my business," Kendall says. "It's none of yours, either."

"Kendall, it *is* my business. It's yours, too. The anniversary of the fire is this Friday. He's got something planned, and it's not a party. Where do you want to be?"

She puts the dish away. "There's nothing we can do."

"I *wish* everyone would stop saying that!"

"What are you saying, Lizbet? That —"

"My name is Gracie."

"Gracie, then. What are we supposed to do? Swim?"

"If I said I could get us out of here, would you come?"

"You can't —"

"Just answer the question."

Kendall hesitates, biting her lip. "I don't know."

"Okay," I say. "That's a start."

THIRTY-TWO

Jonah spends most of Thursday in his part of the house, but I see him from time to time. He pads out in his socks, looks us over, goes back again. There is none of the usual hearty encouragement. None of the beaming smiles. I come to know a particular muscle in his jaw that jumps and quivers, like a burrowing insect under his skin.

I am the one who sees that he is fighting something, and I am the one who knows that if he loses, we lose, too.

Kendall is a reluctant ally, but she is an ally. I move fast before she has a chance to change her mind. I tell her we have to talk to the other kids one by one. Except for Torie and Jeff. Kendall says darkly that they'll never agree, but I just tell her to leave them to me. I just wish I knew what I was going to say to them. The thing is, if they're against it, the plan won't work. They'll see what's up and stop us before I can get it rolling.

We get Dan and Hank to go along by tackling them separately and telling each of them the other one didn't want to go along with the plan. So they both agree. Hank is proud because he has the important role to play. Dan thinks maybe going back to live at his grandmother's house isn't so bad after all, because she has a pool.

I find Tate watching a DVD of some suspense movie. He keeps freezing a frame, then pressing PLAY, then freezing it again. I stop by his chair. Tate is the one boy here who gives off waves of disturbance. His gaze is brittle and hard. I see hurt in his past, deep hurt, starting with him in a crib, and a father standing over him, shouting. I don't want to see what else is there.

I don't want to see anything I've seen inside these kids. I don't want to see the misery and the neglect. I don't want to think about what I'm sending them back to. I just want them to live.

I tell Tate what I think is in Jonah's head. I don't know if he's listening, or if he cares. He stares at the movie, flicking the PAUSE button on and off.

I know better than to try to convince him. I just lay it out.

"Know what God does?" he says. "He sticks it to you. That's what my dad used to say. It's our job to take it and shut up."

I know something about Tate. I've seen how he watches Kendall. I don't want to know what he's thinking. It's another reason to get Kendall out of here. In the meantime, I'll use it.

"Kendall is with me on this," I say. "She thinks we can't do it without you."

I watch his thumb hover over the remote. It hits PLAY.

"Okay," he says.

Maudie and Eli agree because we're older and bigger and seem to know what we're talking about. Eli is used to being told what to do, and Maudie is afraid of being left behind.

It is Ruthanna who surprises me. When I tell her I have a plan to get us all out of here, I don't have to say another word. She lifts her head, her lank hair hanging in her eyes, and says, "My name is Erin. And I'll help."

It is Emily who is the problem. She listens to me lay out the plan, her face a blank.

"No," she says when I finish.

"But Emily . . ."

"He'll kill us," she says.

I exchange a look with Kendall.

"We'll protect you," I say.

"Easy to say. It's not you he wants."

Finally, I say the only thing I can say. "It's all decided. Everyone else has agreed. You'll be safer going along with us."

She looks at me, her face full of fear. But at least it isn't that blankness.

She doesn't say no.

So I take it as a yes.

THIRTY-THREE

Now it's time to tackle Torie and Jeff. If I can get one of them to agree, the other might cave. I decide Jeff will be first.

He flips around the music channels, MTV and BET, all afternoon. Usually with a plate of nachos or potato chips on his lap. The rest of them stay out of his way because if you get between him and the screen, you get yelled at or kicked at.

I sit down on the couch.

He looks over, surprised. No one except Torie ever joins him.

I watch TV with him for a while.

"Can you imagine what people would say if they knew about this?" I ask finally.

Jeff snorts. "Who cares?"

"Think about it. One billionaire, eleven kids, a house full of toys . . . They'd be killing each other to get camera crews in here."

"Yeah," he says. "It'd be wild."

"Katie Couric would be, like, salivating to get your number," I say. "Diane Sawyer would be sending you chocolates. Everybody wants an exclusive, right?"

Jeff doesn't say anything this time. It's a good sign.

"Geez, you think life is sweet in here, imagine what it would be like if you were on the cover of *People,* telling your story." I blow out a breath. "Sheesh."

"*People* magazine is lame," Jeff snorts.

"Of course, you wouldn't want to say too much, because there's the book deal, too. Or the TV movie. They always want to do a TV movie."

He looks at me. "What are you talking about?"

"Who do you think they're going to interview — weird Tate?" I say. "Eli? Ruthanna the mouse? No, they want the smart one. The one with charisma. The one who can tell the story so people will listen. The one who's telegenic."

This gets him thinking. He likes that he's telegenic. His gaze is shrewd now. "What's going on with you?"

"I have a way to get out," I tell him.

He laughs. "You have a death wish."

"It'll work. And once you're out, do you think you're going back on the streets? Into the system? I don't think so. You're going to be famous. The media can't leave this stuff alone. You'd have to play it right, not overexpose yourself. You'd have to be the spokesman of the group, say things right so that you're the one they want to interview. Do you know what a sound bite is?"

"Do you think I'm stupid? I know what it is."

"Sure you do. That's why you'll be the one they want. You know how to feed them the lines."

He drums his fingers on the couch. "What do you think you're going to do? Knock him out? Kill him?"

"We don't have to," I say. "We've got two things on our side. One: There's eleven of us and one of him. Two: He's crazy."

Jeff sniggers. "Tell me something I don't know."

Then he is quiet for a minute.

"So what's your big plan?" he asks casually, and I know I've got him.

Torie is flopped on a couch in the living area playing a Game Boy.

"Get lost," she tells me.

I sit. "I have a plan."

"Good for you. Get lost."

"I know how we can get out of here."

She slowly lowers the Game Boy. Her gaze is murderous. "You are so dead."

"Everyone else is in. Jeff, too," I say deliberately.

I see the tiniest vulnerability in her gaze. Jeff's defection hurts her.

"He wants to be on the cover of *People* magazine," I say.

She laughs. "Yeah. Good luck."

"Here's the insane part," I say. "He *will* be on the cover of *People*. So will you. If you want."

She returns her attention to the Game Boy.

"Everybody's scared," I say.

"Everybody's stupid."

"I think your mom was scared," I say.

Her thumbs stop.

"I think she'd finally found a safe place, and she couldn't give it up."

"What are you talking about?"

"Why she didn't support you when you said that about her boyfriend? About what he did. I think if you'd just hung around just a little more, she would have realized what was true."

She lowers the Game Boy. "I didn't tell anyone here about it. How . . ."

"I just know," I say. "I know the way I know that Jonah is cracking up. That Friday is the day he's been planning for a long time."

"What?"

"You didn't just leave your mom," I say. "You left a life. Friends. Your dad. You didn't even ask him to help."

"He's never helped me before," she mumbles.

"Maybe because you told him you hated him for leaving."

"How do you know this? Did you talk to my dad?"

I shrug. "I'm just telling you. He'll help you."

"What do you *know*?" she yells. Her eyes are dry, but I know the tears are there.

"Living on the street wasn't any better. And no matter what you think, living here isn't, either."

She looks away, biting her lip.

"There's one way to get through," I say. "Tell your story."

"I *told* my story. Nobody believed me."

"Tell it again," I say. "Till someone hears you."

"What if no one does, genius?"

"Someone will," I say. But that is something I can't see, no matter how hard I try.

THIRTY-FOUR

Thursday night is clear. I can see the stars overhead in the skylight. He is on what I've come to think of as his couch, looking through the photo album he's made of all of us. I am across the room on mine.

He passes his fingers across the photographs.

"I worked so hard," he says sadly. "The thing is, I can't let you go."

I take a beat, breathe. I wish like crazy for an adult to be here, someone who knows what they're doing. I have a sudden, immense respect for Dr. Julie Politsky. "I think you can," I say.

"They won't believe that I did a good job. That it all worked."

"We'll tell them," I say.

He brightens. "You'll explain?"

"Of course."

He considers this. Then he shakes his head. He shakes it over and over. "No. No. They still won't get it." He sits and clasps his hands.

"You ran onto the beach," I say, prompting him. "You were barefoot."

He looks up. The moon casts a bone-cold light on his face. "He wanted to bury Nell here. I couldn't let him do that. He wanted all of us, the children, to bury her. Even the little ones. To dig the grave. I couldn't let him do that. They were so scared. So I used the radio. I sent a distress signal."

"And he saw you."

"He chased me outside."

"Did he catch you?"

He looks up at the moon and doesn't answer. Then he reaches into his pocket, takes out his card, and enters something. Slowly, the skylights close. Now there is nothing but darkness. It's suddenly hard for me to breathe.

"I saw the flames from the beach," Jonah says dreamily. "I ran. When I got closer, I heard the pounding."

The pounding on the door. The father had locked them in.

"What did you do?"

"I broke the window. The ones in the front, they got out. It wasn't too bad yet. I was looking for you."

For Lizbet.

"Some of us got out. We all said it was an accident. To protect him. After that, we left the island. We moved up north, near the border."

He looks at me. "You understand, don't you? I had to show them how it's done. And they won't get it."

I see now. I thought the *they* he talked about had

been the public, the media, the world at large. But *they* are two particular people — his parents. He is trying to show his *parents* how to make a family.

"Here's the ironic thing," he says. "After all this, I see that he was right after all. I understand him now. I've lived his life. He couldn't bear to be separated from us. Isn't that the definition of a good father? I thought I could save you all by giving you love. But it's not enough. It won't keep us together. People grow up, you know. People disobey. People want to leave. Isn't that funny, that I forgot that? *I* was the one to disobey. *I* was the one who wanted to leave. I've come this far and I've made a circle. I've made a circle. But I can still make it right this time."

I understand it now. He blames himself for everything. For Nell's death, because he didn't send the distress signal soon enough. For the fire, because he sent the distress signal at all. He had pushed his father past desperation into madness. His father had set the fire and locked his family in, because he couldn't bear to have them taken away.

And now it's up to me. I've spent all day preparing for this moment.

"Nell never had a birthday party," I say.

"No."

"We should do that. We should give her a party this time. Do it right this time."

This catches him. He turns to me and his gaze is brighter.

"Yes," he says. "This time I'll get it right."

"She didn't want to say anything," I say. "You know how she is."

"Of course."

"We should do something."

"Well, of course, that's what we should do. We have to bake a cake!"

"Of course," I say.

"Frances will sing. And Tate will play guitar."

"Susannah and I will bake the cake."

"Cool!"

"And Eli and Maudie will make the decorations. A family celebration."

"I can't wait," he says. The look of childish anticipation on his face makes me turn away.

THIRTY-FIVE

Naturally, Torie is no help with baking the cake, but I find the recipe book and manage to do it. I even find birthday candles. Long ago, Jonah had stocked the closet with paper plates and party hats, but the kids say that they never celebrated birthdays before. If they remembered their birthdays, they kept it to themselves.

Tate sets up the projection screens in the dining room. Everything is ready to go.

Everyone has a job to do.

And now everything just has to go as planned.

This is our best shot.

Maybe our only shot.

Because if we fail . . . I don't want to think about if we fail.

It is four o'clock when we call the others to the table. It looks festive, with streamers and paper plates. Jonah has a party hat on. He pokes his head in the kitchen. "Is the cake ready?"

"Yes."

"Should I get Nell? I'll get her."

He ducks out again. He is sixteen again. He is

going to get his sister, to take her to the party she never had.

He is that far gone. He has no sense now of who we really are. He is in a place that is somewhere between the past and the present.

We turn out all the lights. Torie is ready in the kitchen, the others ready to run to the bedrooms and playroom. Hank is behind the door. Tate is ready by the computer.

Jonah leads her in. Emily looks terrified. Frozen.

"Come on," he says, urging her. "It's a surprise."

She shakes her head, not moving.

"Get in there," Torie hisses to me. "The wacko is going to blow it."

I burst in with the cake. We sing "Happy Birthday." I try to give Emily courage with my gaze, but hers keeps sliding away.

Tate flips on the projections. The screens light up with a summer rainstorm. The rain is rhythmic. It would be soothing, but Tate has pumped up the volume.

Jonah stops singing. "Stop it! Stop it!" he shouts. "Turn off the rain!"

Tate turns up the volume.

"No!" Jonah yells.

Emily is supposed to take his hand now. That was the plan. She doesn't do it.

Hank moves toward Jonah. Emily remains standing still. She covers her ears with her hands as Jonah yells to turn down the rainstorm.

"Now!" I yell, and we scatter.

We all count in our heads as we run. One. Two. Three. Four. Five. They are running to the computers, to the space heaters in the bathrooms. I run to the dishwasher, Torie to the two ovens. Six. Seven. Eight. Jonah is shouting, but it's just noise now. Nine. Ten.

At the same moment, we flip on everything we can. Torie cranks the oven to five hundred degrees and switches on all the burners. I switch on the dishwasher to its hottest setting. Maudie has started the three dryers. In the bathrooms, the heaters are on, the blow-dryers for the girls' hair. In the playrooms, the TVs, the computers, the stereo.

The generator blows.

We are plunged into darkness.

I push open the door to the dining area. I can see faintly by the light coming from the skylight in the living room. Jonah is whirling, shouting. Emily has dropped to the floor, out of sight, rolled into a ball. Hank is moving, dressed in black jeans and a black T-shirt, almost invisible. I see the gleam of his hand as he slips it into Jonah's front pocket. Emily was supposed to prevent Jonah from grabbing Hank by distracting him, but she didn't. Jonah turns, but he doesn't feel Hank's hand, he just sees him.

"What are you doing?" he says to Hank. "Where's Nell?"

Hank hands off the card to Jeff and they are running now, running toward the front door.

"Where are you going? It's her party! What's happening?" Jonah screams.

I run forward and drop to the floor. *"Go,"* I tell Emily.

She is frozen. She shakes her head.

"Emily, listen." I plead. I grab her face. *"We have something to go back to."*

Her expression changes slightly, but her arms are still locked around her legs. She ducks her head down.

I physically push down her legs, unwind her arms. I scream for Kendall. Together, we pull Emily out from under the table.

"Go," I say, pushing her.

And somehow her legs move, and she goes, Kendall half-pulling her.

The other kids are running to the front door, where Jeff is swiping the lock. There is a backup generator, but I know it takes a few minutes to kick on. Maybe five. Maybe more if we're lucky.

I run to the front door. Hank puts the card in my hand. Jeff is already out the door with Torie.

Hank looks hesitant. "I'll come with you."

"No. You have to get them on the boat. If I'm not there in five minutes, just go."

"Gracie . . ."

I can hear Jonah behind me, bellowing like an animal. He is tearing the house apart, looking for Emily. Looking for Nell in order to save her again.

I will be alone in the house with him. The fear of that is in my mouth, in my stomach. I've never felt so afraid.

"Go," I say to Hank, and push him out the door.

THIRTY-SIX

I run through the dark house, dodging the furniture. I race down the hallway toward the door to Jonah's wing. He is in the playroom. I tell myself I have time enough to do this.

My hands are shaking so badly that I can't swipe the card. I fumble and drop it. I hear him move from the playroom into the big living area. I swipe the card, and the light glows green. I push the door open.

I run down a short hallway. His bedroom door is open. There is a twin bed with a blanket, a chest of drawers, and a wall crammed with computer equipment. Hank has told me where the panel is. I race to it and swipe the card, getting it right the first time. The light shifts to green and I open the panel.

My fingers scrabble down the neatly lettered spaces.

SECURITY WALL. I turn the switch from ON to OFF.

BOATHOUSE SECURITY. OFF.

His arms are suddenly around me, around my waist, and he lifts me up as though I am a doll and throws me. I land hard on my knees. He drags me by one arm. I am screaming at him to stop, the pain is so bad in my arm, but he's not hearing me. His gaze is cloudy; his face is red with panic and rage.

Suddenly, he throws himself down on the rug next to me. I smell smoke again, but this time I know it's real.

"Lizbet," he says, curling up next to me, holding me down with one arm. "This time I won't leave you."

The generator kicks in, and the lights come on. I see his face, his unseeing eyes. I cringe when he strokes my hair.

I get a flash of his stroking his sister's hair. They are lying on the floor, waiting to die.

Smoke is in the room, and Lizbet is coughing.

Suddenly, Jonah raises his head.

He tries to pull Lizbet, but she slumps down.

He sees something — a light? He crawls toward it.

And I am back again here, with my head on the rug, and Jonah's hand on my head.

A moment ago, all that was in my mind was a scream. I couldn't focus or think. Now I know the only way out of this is to think.

"You left me last time," I say.

He ducks his head to my shoulder. "I'm sorry. I came back inside to get you. I didn't realize it would be so bad. I had to get out. This time I won't leave without you. This time I'll do it right."

That's it, I think. I have it now. This time, he won't be the one to get out. Getting it right means he'll stay with Lizbet. Stay in the fire.

"Let's go out together," I say. I can't see the fire, I can't feel it, but I can smell it and the panic is shivering up my legs.

He raises his head and looks into my face tenderly. "I won't leave you."

"Jonah, please," I beg. "Please."

"You are my family," he says. "Let's just go to sleep."

The smoke is in my lungs now.

I press my face down as far as I can, to find air.

I can't breathe.

I cough and cough. My lungs are filling up with blood.

My lungs are filling up with smoke.

Smoke and blood.

My mother is dying.

Lizbet is dying.

I am dying.

They burst back in the room then, all the kids, every one of them. My face is pushed into the carpet.

I'm coughing, but there is no smoke in the room.

But the smell is real. The fire is in another part of the house.

Torie grabs Jonah's arm, Hank grabs the other, Jeff grabs him by the neck, and all together they pull him off me. He kicks and screams like a child, bawling, his face red, but they manage to hold him back until I'm on my feet.

They drop him, and we run for the door. He's on his knees, struggling to get up.

Somehow we scramble through the door. Smoke is hanging in the living area. We run to the front door.

The fresh air is a relief. It is a surprise to me to see that the sun is shining. That seems the strangest thing of all.

The door is open in the wall, and we race through it. He is still running after us, running across the beach barefoot, as we reach the boat-house door. They've propped it open, they were smart. We race down the dock, jump into the boat.

Torie gets behind the wheel. "Does anyone know how to drive this thing?"

He's on the deck now, pounding toward us. "Don't go!" he roars. "Don't go! Please!"

Tate jumps into the pilot seat and turns the key that is dangling from the lock. He does something else and the boat begins to move. Jonah jumps from the deck, his arms whirling, his legs pumping. We feel his hands slap the boat and then the boat is moving and he goes under.

Jonah appears above the water. The wake of the boat slaps him in the face. His mouth is open, sucking in air, sobbing.

He howls.

His gaze locks on mine. "You're my *family*!" he shouts.

"I have a family," I whisper as the boat chugs out to the open sea.

THIRTY-SEVEN

This time, it is me who hears the footsteps, hears the sob that escapes despite the hand pressed against it, trying to hold it in. I lay awake, listening, as Shay moves down the hall. The door squeaks as she enters the kitchen. I can't hear the birds yet, but I can just make out the trees outside my window.

I've been back for a week now. A week of eating and sleeping and not answering the phone. Shay took the week off from work. It's the biggest story to hit Seattle since . . . well, since anyone can remember.

There was a compass on board, so we headed east, hoping we'd bump into land before we ran out of gas. We saw the ferry before they saw us, and we found the flares in the emergency kit. At first, it was just logistics. Calling parents, getting back to Seattle. Then the media storm broke on us the next day. We woke up famous.

Emily's parents took her away, down south to Rocky's sister in Portland. Torie and Jeff have been on *Good Morning America,* the *Today* show, and I hear they'll be on the cover of *People* next week. They are heroes. The oldest kids who protected the rest of us. They are getting everything they wanted, and I wish them well with celebrity. Somehow I doubt they'll be able to handle it.

All the rest of the kids have landed back at home — like Kendall — or in social services — like Tate.

They found Jonah waiting on the beach, sitting barefoot, staring out to sea, the house still smoking behind him.

He had started out with street kids. Maybe in the beginning he was really trying to help them. Torie and Jeff were the first. Then he started contacting kids on the Internet. He'd make sure they answered him in cyber-cafés and didn't tell their parents. When he found out that Emily had written him on her computer, he'd made her take it with her when she came to meet him. Because Beewick Island was so small, he wiped the library computers himself. Emily let him into Rocky's and he wiped Zed's computer, too, because Emily had used it. He had gotten sloppy with Emily, because she could be traced through the computer camp, and Kendall had already disappeared. So he asked his publicity department to remove her from the photos, just in case one got into the Seattle papers and triggered a link.

The board of Jonah's company has hired the best defense team in the country, and it looks like they'll plead the insanity defense.

I told Shay and Diego all about it, or about most of it. I couldn't tell them the way Jonah ate away at my insides, the way he made me hurt. But I think they knew. Diego got in about fifty pounds of trouble for taking me to the park that day. I don't think Shay had forgiven him until I came back.

I don't think Diego had forgiven himself, either. It turned out that one of those three-year-olds in the park had gotten lost and hysterical, and by the time Diego returned the little boy to one of the nature walk instructors, I was gone.

I think Shay must have lost ten pounds while I was away, and she doesn't even mention it. I'll never forget the look on her face when she walked into the room at the Seattle police station. I'll never forget how she held me, like I belonged to her, like losing me would have killed her. I didn't know she felt that way.

I swing my legs over the bed. I pad outside to the kitchen. Shay is sitting at the kitchen table with a wadded up tissue in her hand. She's staring out at the darkness. A pot of milk is on the stove on a low flame.

"So did you and Mom become blonds?" I ask, sitting down.

Shay's eyes are red-rimmed. Her mouth is taut from crying, from trying not to cry. I see raw grief on her face, and it stuns me. She's been hiding it from me, I realize. She didn't want to add to mine.

She had let me know, in a thousand ways, how much she missed my mom, but she never let me see her pain. I'm not sure if that was the right way to go, but I understand.

She clears her throat. "Carrie looked fantastic. Like she'd spent a month in the sun. I wanted to look just like her, so I left it on too long. It came out sort of platinum, and not in a good way. So we tried to dye it back, and it sort of looked greenish. So she looks at me, and she says, 'Maybe we should try on hats.' I just remember lying on the bath-room floor, laughing so hard. She could laugh so hard . . ."

"She would totally lose control."

Shay looks down at her hands. "You know, I just remembered this. I said something about how we'd have to learn to dye our own hair because we'd have to get rid of the gray when we got older, and Carrie said, 'I'll never have gray hair.' She said it totally seriously. I thought she meant she'd be lucky. But now I wonder if . . ."

"If she knew she'd never get old. If she was . . . like me."

"Maybe that's why she was always in such a hurry to live her life."

I absorb this. I wonder what it would be like, feeling that you wouldn't live long. I realize there are parts to my mom that I didn't know, deep parts, quirky parts. It's not just my memories that define her. Shay lost her, too. I want to hear those memories now. Now I'm ready to listen.

Shay gets up and pours out the hot milk. She's made enough for two, just in case.

"Do you ever . . . sense her?" she asks. I can tell this is hard for her to get out. And I can tell how badly she wants me to say yes.

"No," I say. "It doesn't work that way. There's absolutely nothing good about being psychic that I can see. It's a curse."

She takes a sharp, indrawn breath as she breaks up the chocolate into two mugs and brings them to the table. Then she pours in the milk. We stir, our spoons gently tinkling.

"You got ten kids out of hell because of it. That's good."

"It almost didn't happen that way."

"But it did." Shay blows on her drink. "You can use it. Not let it use you. That's all I'm saying."

We take a sip at the same moment, and swallow.

"Do you still get flashes of him?" Shay asks.

I shake my head firmly. "Not new ones." The memory of what he had done and seen is enough to keep me awake at night. The memories of the kids I tapped into gave me a glimpse into a world I didn't want to know, a place where love had withered at its root.

It's going to take me time.

"Loss can stretch you into a new shape," Shay

says. "Jonah was handed too much, and he didn't have the foundation to handle it. He couldn't find a way to live that made sense."

I take my first sip. I like it like this, when the chocolate has just started to melt, when I taste milk and just the beginning of the sweetness.

"You'll always be sad, Gracie," Shay says. "That doesn't mean you'll never be happy."

"Yeah," I say.

The light is changing. It is blue, bluer than blue. We hear the birds begin to squawk.

"By the way," I tell her, "Joe Fusilli has a crush on you."

A small smile curves her lips. "Yeah?"

She props her bare feet up on the sill. I put my feet next to hers. I remember the day I stared at her feet and transferred all my hatred onto her toes. Now I see how her foot is shaped like mine, how her toes are all almost the same size, like mine. I hold the warm cup cradled against my chest. In his loony way, Jonah was right about something.

You just can't get away from family.

More Cool Reads

DAVID KLASS

Funny, gritty and **unquestionably compelling**

'It's fast-paced, moving and at times very funny –
parts of it made me laugh out loud'
– Louis Sacher, author of Holes

'A novel you will remember for a long time'
– Guardian on You Don't Know Me

MEG ROSOFF

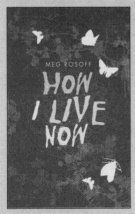

A breathtaking, deeply romantic debut novel of love, war and a family torn apart

'That rare, rare thing, a first novel with a sustained, magical and utterly faultless voice. After five pages I knew that she could persuade me to believe almost anything'

– Mark Haddon, author of The Curious Incident of the Dog in the Night-Time

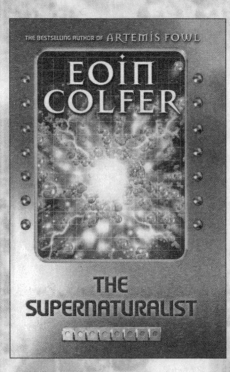

ROBERT CORMIER

Fear seeps
through the pages

Uncompromising thrillers
from the
master of suspense

DAY IS RULED BY DOGS.
NIGHT BELONGS TO THE RATS.

BUT IN-BETWEEN is DUSK'S TIME...

Dusk, the product of a military experiment to fuse human and hawk DNA, has earned her place as one of the top predators. But then Jay, the boy, stumbles into the deserted town. He's food for the predators.

If the dogs don't get him, the rats will. Is Dusk human enough to help him? And can he help save her?

ROBERT SWINDELLS

Heart-racing,

bone-chilling,

jaw-dropping

THRILLERS.